One Hand Screaming

Mark Leslie

Thanks for the hand Uncle! Thinking about you.

STARK
PUBLISHING

Stark Publishing

August 2004

Copyright © 2004 Mark Leslie Lefebvre

"Til Death Do Us Part" © 2004 Mark Leslie Lefebvre & John David Strickland
"It Creeps Up On You" © 2004 Mark Leslie Lefebvre & Carol Weekes

Cover design by Stephan Gaydos
Cover art by Agnes Bartlett
Author photograph by Greg Roberts

"Browsers" first appeared in Challenging Destiny; "Distractions" & "It Creeps Up On You" first appeared in World Fantasy Con 2001 CD-Rom; "From Out of the Night" first appeared in The Darker Woods, "Nervous Twitching", "Frost After Midnight", "There is a Low & Fearful Cry" & "Blood Dreams" first appeared in NorthWords; "The Bogeyman Can" first appeared in imelod; "With Apologies to E.P." first appeared in Twisted Devotion; "Wailin Jenny" first appeared in Thin Ice; "Holiday Demons", "But Once A Year", "Treats" & "Tricky Treater" first appeared in Crossroads; "Phantom Mitch" first appeared in Wicked Mystic; "Erratic Cycles" first appeared in Parsec; "Requiem" first appeared in Darkness Within; "That Old Silk Hat They Found" first appeared in Strange Wonderland

Visit Stark Publishing on the web at www.starkpublishing.ca

ISBN 0-973-56880-1

Printed in the United States of America

For Carol Weekes and John Strickland – collaborating and working with each of you has been a pleasure, an inspiration and has taught me how to be a better writer

And for Francine – collaborating with you on this life journey is an experience that I treasure beyond words and which continually teaches me how to be a better person.

Acknowledgements

While the title of this book reflects an activity performed by one individual, it is not without the constant support, encouragement, assistance, guidance and friendship of others.

Ken Abner, David Barnett, Don Bassie, Richard Blair, James Botte, Cathy Buburuz, Joseph Cherkes, Martha Closs, Stephanie Connolly, Sean Costello, Julie E. Czerneda, Ellen Datlow, Bertrand Desbiens, John Ellis, Melanie E. Fischer, Todd H. C. Fischer, Jack Fisher, Denise Fleischer, Sandra Fritz, Gary Fuhrman, Steve Gaydos, Charles Grant, Paul Griffin, Peter Halasz, Christine Harkness, Brian A. Hopkins, Rob Howard, Don Hutchison, Rebecca Anne Jansen, Kathleen Jurgens, Sandra Kasturi, Nancy Kilpatrick, Ed Kobialka, Chris Krejlgaard, Chris Lacher, Richard Laymon, Christie Leblanc, Stan Lee, Timothy Libby, Sally McBride, Mary Maccusi, Elizabeth Martin-Burk, Arianne Matte, Pete Mihajic, Pat Nielsen, Michelle Norry, David O'Meara, Neil Peart, Greg Roberts, Robert J. Sawyer, Andre Scheluchin, Dale L Sproule, Taki Stewart, John Strickland, David M. Switzer, Jim Turcott, Edo van Belkom, Dean Watson, Carol Weekes . . .

. . . have all either published my writing, or are people whose own creativity, friendship or insightful comments have helped make me better at my craft. While I've attempted to name them all, this is but the small part of that iceberg which is visible.

Special Gratitude to: Greg Roberts, for the author photo; Steve Gaydos, for the design and layout of the cover; Sean Costello, for creative assistance, input and insight into the collection; Dianne Marzanek, for use of her mother's artwork on the cover, and of course, for her beautiful daughter.

Thanks to Mom & Baba who, although not always enamoured with the subject matter for most of my creative efforts, still put up my drawings of monsters when I was a child and supported the idea that I wanted to be a writer. And to Dad whose creativity in woodworking and link to nature was a constant inspiration and whose memory and love still burns strong in my heart.

Thanks, Alexander, my beautiful son, whom I cradled in one arm while doing the final work on this book. You're a miracle who inspires me in a way I could never imagine before. I love you, little one.

And as always, I could not do any of what I do without the unwavering and tireless support and love of my wife Francine. I love you, Lamb-kabob.

TABLE OF CONTENTS

SILENT SCREAMS
A Note From The Author

I SCREAM A LOT.

Silent screams bounce around inside my head like an impending storm brewing into a force that will escape in a wild dance of chaos and be lost forever if I don't stop to jot them down.

I'm a condemned man. Condemned to write.

But don't get me wrong; I love it.

For centuries, philosophers have been plagued with the question: "What is the sound of one hand clapping?" But, due to my curse, my deeper, more morbid musings, I am doomed to consider: *What is the sound of one hand screaming?* Why ask? Why delve into the darkness? Why pursue fear and terror?

There's really no answer. I merely respond to a call both from within and from without. Human beings have been eagerly devouring notions of evil and horror since we dwelt in caves and jumped at the shadows and noises occurring just outside the comforting range of firelight. History is wrought with examples of people standing alone, facing a vast, empty void and questioning both themselves and the universe.

Canadians, especially, have always been concerned with notions of what lies beyond our normal existence. From the days when we had still to explore the uncharted west and northern territories to a time when our very cities seem to be a futile attempt to light up the dark, we are both intrigued with and fearful of the unknown.

ONE HAND SCREAMING

One Hand Screaming explores one man's journey into the unknown and dealing with such universal elements. At a basic level, it documents the early evolution of a writer cursed to churn out morbid musings, spin dark tales that question the ideas of evil and of sanity. It is a collection of fiction and poetry, but it can also be seen in an autobiographical sense if you decide to read the final chapter of story notes. I purposely separated them from the stories and poems to ensure that those readers who prefer not to "see the strings" behind the writing can simply skip them and still enjoy the tales.

But regardless of how you choose to enjoy this work, I trust that if you try really hard, you'll be able to hear, almost out of perceptible range, a series of silent screams.

Don't worry – it's just me.

I scream a lot.

Mark Leslie, February 2004

MARK LESLIE

THE SOUND OF ONE MAN SCREAMING

☠

BROWSERS

*"The stimulation of seeing so many books so suddenly seemed
almost more than was good for the frail little boy."*
-George R. Stewart, Earth Abides

STEPPING INTO a used book shop is sometimes like stepping into
another dimension. Where else but a used book store can one find
such an eclectic selection of minds and experiences stored in dusty
tomes, just waiting to be browsed through by anyone who happens
along?

Occasionally a used book shop can be a painful experience,
offering up nothing more than the latest trashy paperbacks and adult
porn magazines.

But sometimes . . .

Sometimes a used book store can provide, to the avid browser, a
mystical experience. Sometimes, walking through that door, you are
overwhelmed with a sense of awe, a sense that something powerful is
being housed within the very walls.

I discovered such a wondrous shop years ago on the corner of
two streets whose names I cannot remember in one of those pseudo-
cities on the south western edge of the Golden Horseshoe.

Standing on the street, the sounds of traffic all around me, I
beheld the quaint corner shop with curious eyes. The dark and dusty
windows did not allow me a clear view of the interior of the shop, and
apart from the word BROWSERS painted on the window there was
no exterior sign indicating the name of the establishment.

Trying to remember if I'd been to this particular shop before, I opened the door. The tiny bell overhead tinkled as I stepped inside. I had to pause as the familiar feeling of awe overtook me. Perhaps you feel it, too, when you walk into a used book shop – the feeling that all eternity is poised, trapped in the moment, just waiting to spill forth into the future.

Literature has always fascinated me. With writing, humankind has developed the ability to elevate a person to a state of immortality. And with that, anyone who reads can thus share in that immortal bliss. None of us have ever had the pleasure of meeting Shakespeare or Dickens personally, but they are still companions in our day to day travels. Though long dead, they are very much with us. That is the beauty and power of literature.

Perhaps that is why I had spent the last three decades of my life writing, trying to capture the spirit of myself on paper. To that point, I had been unsuccessful, forced to live vicariously through the bold efforts of those great masters who'd come before me.

That is probably why I would take such pleasure in browsing through a used book shop. And occasionally, when feeling daring, I would fantasize about future generations browsing such a shop and finding one of my works – essentially discovering my spirit and thus keeping me alive.

The absence of a book clerk was the first thing I noticed. But that wasn't unusual. He or she could be shelving books or helping another customer. Standing in the tiny entranceway I glanced at the small podium desk, which I assumed the owner used as a work space. My eyes then led forward to the next connected room which was perhaps eight by twelve feet. I moved into it. This room, crammed with the usual variety of books, led off directly to another room of similar size.

Trying to get my bearings, I searched through the second room to find two more doorways to a third and forth room. I took the door on the right and found, from that room, another three choices.

The peculiarity struck me at that point. I paused and breathed in my amazement. What looked like such a tiny corner shop was actually a huge space divided into a multitude of rooms.

I saw myself spending a lot of time here.

I decided to waste no more time and began my browsing. I turned and scanned the books that filled the room I stood in. The shelves reached all the way up to the nine foot ceiling of the room and were packed, tightly, with all sorts of books. Scanning the titles, I noticed that there was no particular order to them. There was an abundance of westerns and the occasional thriller shelved in this room; but apart from that, there was a plethora of every other imaginable type of book. From a selection of children's picture books to a sampling of cheap dime paperbacks, this room had it all. On the far wall sat a selection of magazines and comic books. Beside that were stacks of yellowed newspapers.

"What an interesting setup," I muttered, and my voice carried strangely through the room. My words broke a silence so thick, I might have been standing in an ancient Egyptian tomb. I turned, as if trying to catch my words and take them back so that I might not wake the sleeping texts. But alas, my words were out and lost to me forever.

As I turned I looked through the entrance to another room I hadn't seen before, and a paperback book spine leapt out at me as if highlighted. I stepped into that room and plucked the book from the shelf. It was one of my favourites from a long time back. George R. Stewart's *Earth Abides*. I held it in my hand like a trophy.

I thumbed it open and sniffed at the wonderfully musty smell that can hardly be described so much as it is loved by a bibliophile. Then I flipped through to the middle of the book and began reading, but not aloud. I dared not speak anything else aloud for fear of ruining, again, that special silence.

I read a passage that had stuck with me all these years. The main character, Ish, upon rebuilding a small civilization after the world had been ravaged by plague, takes the boy Joey to one of the libraries left over from before Year One.

Halfway through this scene I noticed that certain words from this passage were missing, as if the ink from the page had dissolved. I flipped through to another passage. Sure enough, the same thing seemed to have happened there as well.

I put the book down and picked up another one. Again, several passages throughout that text were blank – in some places complete lines were missing. I tried another to find the same results, randomly scattered throughout.

I paused and sniffed the air, as if I would be able to tell if there were some corrosive elements lurking in the room, slowly removing the ink from the pages. But I could detect nothing.

Instead, I left the books there and moved on into the next room to my right. I selected another paperback and noticed that none of the words were missing from it. I replaced it and moved across the room, grabbing at what appeared to be an old SOCIOLOGY text. Strangely, whole pages and entire chapters were blank.

I had heard stories and read articles stating that the paper itself of some of the oldest books printed were apparently reacting with the air, causing them to disintegrate. I wondered if perhaps a similar thing was happening, here, but to the ink rather than the paper.

Such a thought sent shivers through my being. The books in these rooms were not ancient by any means, and already the words were dissolving to nothing. A discovery like this might seem happenstance to the average person, or perhaps boring to one whose only source of information is the Internet; but to a book lover like myself, it was as if God had stepped down from heaven and announced that the world would soon be ending.

I spent the next ten minutes or so rushing from room to room, picking up different types of books and thumbing through them, trying to discover some sort of pattern. But the dissolution of the words seemed completely random. It wasn't specific to any one room, or any one kind of book – the phenomenon appeared without any detectable pattern.

It then came upon me to try to find the book clerk and point my discovery out to him or her. Or perhaps the book clerk would already have known about this strange occurrence. Perhaps they would explain it to me as a result of the nearby industrial smelters filling the local atmosphere with a highly selective airborne corrosive material.

Only, by that point, I could not quite remember the way I had come. I began a path from room to room, hoping I'd recall having been in one of them. But in the same way that I was unable to detect a pattern in the phenomenon of the dissolving words, I was also unable to recognize any of the rooms I'd passed through.

I called out, once, only to hear my voice echo through the room I was in and bounce out in the many available directions. But, as before when I spoke, I had the strange sensation that my voice would wake the sleeping tomes.

Beginning to panic, I ran. From room to room I ran, first taking every exit to my immediate right, and, when that didn't help, every doorway to my left.

Finally, I collapsed to the floor, out of breath and out of the energy to be panicked any longer. It looks like I might be trapped here for a long time, I told myself. I might as well take my time and map out my movement in the maze of books and rooms – perhaps that would help me.

I pulled a hardback text from the wall and flipped through it until I found a blank page. Digging into the breast pocket of my jacket, I plucked out my Mont Blanc pen – the one I always carried with me. Perhaps it was in case I was overcome with that once-in-a-lifetime inspiration that all aspiring writers dream will come. Perhaps it was a ritual of connecting myself with a writing instrument so that we were mates on the voyage of life. Whatever it was, I was glad to have made the effort, my whole adult life, to carry this pen with me. For that day, it just might be the thing that helped me get out of this unusual dilemma.

I began to scribble down the shape of the room that I was standing in, leaving spaces to the front of myself, to my left and directly behind me where the other rooms joined it. Then, my sketch of that room complete, I entered the room directly in front of me.

A hollow groan boomed through the infinite silence.

The groan steadily became a wail as I paused in the doorway, dropping both pen and book to clamp my hands to my ears. It echoed through my head despite my efforts to keep it out and seemed to swirl around the room, announcing its misery in no uncertain terms.

Then, as suddenly as it had begun, it stopped.

I turned on the spot, almost afraid to see what had caused that horrid sound. But there was nothing in the room behind me. Nothing, of course, but the books and the shelves that had always been there.

There was no way I was going to go back into that room. Whatever caused that sound might be lurking around the corner. I considered my pen and the book I'd dropped just inside the room, and decided to abandon my plans of mapping out the place.

I then wandered, almost casually considering how startled I'd been, from room to room. Occasionally, I would stop to examine a book which caught my eye. I did this – according to my wristwatch – for about three hours.

During this time I discovered a couple more abnormalities. The first notable one was that a good deal of the books I examined lacked a copyright page. I wasn't sure whether to chalk it up to the same phenomenon that caused the ink to disappear or if it was for some other reason.

The second was the physical layout of the rooms. I mentioned earlier that the shelves reached right up to the ceiling, but I believe I failed to note the differing heights of each room. Each room conformed to a slightly different shape and height, almost the way each snowflake is not exactly the same as the next, no matter how similar they at first appear.

It was towards the end of this casual wandering when I was struck with a strange notion. I thought about all the books I'd seen that day which I would love to have purchased. The only problem was that I couldn't find the cashier. How ironic to have such a wonderful choice of books and be unable to purchase any. Not only that, but for the most part to discover, upon beginning to take the time to read the book, that it was not actually.

I wondered, for a moment, if I had died and was somehow in a kind of hell for book browsers. The ones who waltz into a store, browse for hours, even sit and read entire chapters and then leave, never once making a single purchase. I laughed at the irony of such a hell and then decided against it. Having worked at a bookstore for my first four years after graduating from college, I knew that if this were such a hell, not only would I not be alone here, but there would barely be room for us all, no matter how endless these rooms seemed.

Still, it was an interesting premise to toss about in my mind while tried to find my way out. Several such notions gnawed at me in the hours I wandered, before I was finally overcome with fatigue and had to sit.

Not long after propping myself up against a bookshelf I must have fallen asleep.

☠   ☠   ☠

I'm not sure how long after that I awoke – but when I did, it felt like no other waking I'd ever experienced. I could still sense the world around me, but I wasn't quite myself anymore.

As best I can describe, I was nothing more than a room stacked with shelf upon shelf of all the books I had read in my life. I was added onto the maze of rooms in this "book shop" and must have somehow been fused into it while I slept.

I can't really say how this happened or who caused it. At least now I understand a little of the weird phenomenon which I had discovered, for it occurs in the books which I house inside of me – inside of the special room which is me.

I hold inside of me all of the texts which I have read over the course of my life. And within those texts are certain words, passages and entire pages which I either skipped over, or which I accidentally missed while reading them. So it wasn't due to some strange chemical in the air, but rather from a reading habit which can occur in even the most fastidious reader.

My consciousness is mostly taken up by the books within my spirit. And being stuck only with them, I am sad that I had not read them more carefully while I'd had the chance. For I have perused them again, countless times. And yes, I am disappointed for having accidentally or intentionally skipped certain parts, for I never will know the words I had missed out on.

As time passes, though, and I'm not sure how much has, I am slowly learning how to extend my consciousness out into the neighbouring rooms and peruse any of the same texts my silent companions have read that I might house, hoping to fill in the gaps of my own books. It takes what seems like eternity and quite a bit of concentrated effort, but it can be done. After all, it's not like I don't have the time. My only problem is that I fear the time when that too will not be enough.

What we need is more. We need more things to read and share with each other. And we wait for that day when one will join us who has read all the same books we have but who has also read *all* the words so we might be enlightened completely.

We have nothing but time, so we wait.

Oh, but soft, I think I hear the entrance bell tinkling. Could it be? Yes, I think it is.

After all this time of browsing through countless bookstores, you have found your rightful resting place. Nice of you to come. Browse to your heart's content. We've been waiting a long time for you to join us.

DISTRACTIONS

MAXWELL WASN'T surprised when the rubber ball smashed through the window and rolled to a stop near his feet. In fact, he hardly flinched as the shards of glass flew through the air, some of them nesting in his blond curly locks.

He'd known it was only a matter of time before the ball being bounced against the side of the house strayed just enough to hit the window.

Maxwell looked down at the signed copy of Andy Robinson's latest self-help bestseller: MAXIM POWER II: GETTING THROUGH DISTRACTIONS. Andy's proud, smiling face (with his unique trademark oversized cleft chin and dimples) on the cover brought the book's first words to his mind.

Distractions should be seen as evil.

Calmly, Maxwell picked up the ball and walked out of the study. The ball was made of Indian rubber, warm and hard with just a little give as he pressed his thumb into it. Tossing the ball into the air and catching it with the same hand, he headed down the hall on his way to the door.

The packed book shelf at the end of the hall caught his eye, as it often did. He paused to run the tips of his fingers across the spines of the books. His fingers stopped on a book with golden lettering down the spine reading: THE BRAZEN HERALD.

He pulled the book off the shelf, admiring the cover lettering, the artwork, the dark winged-dragon silhouette against a purple-red sky, and below that, a blue-black sea, and the lone figure standing in the foreground on the edge of the cliff, mostly in silhouette, the blue and yellow tunic showing, the glinting shine of the sword in hand. Turning the hardcover book in his hand, he admired the black and white photo on the back, how the smiling face captured there resembled him, yet was different. A fuller head of hair, the confident smile of an author still producing. Then he read the text. 'Maxwell Bronte lives with his wife Doris in Arizona and is hard at work on his next novel, furthering the chronicles of Sebastian Eldritch.' He smiled and fondly remembered those days. The novel had been praised and cheered – he had been the talk of the town, described as *that up and coming fantasy writer from the Southwest*, the way that King was the horror writer from New England. He'd been interviewed and featured in all the major Science Fiction & Fantasy journals.

That, of course, had been five years ago. He still hadn't finished the follow up novel about Sebastian Eldritch, the one he had been planning on calling HERALD IN PERIL. No, between that first blockbuster novel and now, he'd gone through two job changes, the loss of his father, a near divorce and a house fire. Getting back to working on his novel had not been a priority during those changes.

The world around you shouldn't decide your priorities for you. Only you can do that.

Until he discovered Andy Robinson, that was, and learned that all of it, all that change, turmoil and upset, was really nothing more than distractions that had been getting in the way of fulfilling his destiny.

He'd bumped into Andy at *Roc*Kon*, a science fiction convention in Little Rock just a few months ago. Maxwell was still touring the conventions, riding on his one past publishing success and hoping to revitalize his career by being around other successful authors. He'd ended up reminding himself of a certain television star from 20 years ago whose soul quest seemed to be to work non-stop at rallying fans to help bring back STARSHIP ACADEMY, despite the fact that most of the other main cast members from that series had either all but disappeared from acting or had died.

Minutes after making that realization and wondering if he would be doing this for another fifteen years, he'd gotten off the elevator at the wrong floor, where he'd stumbled into a business leaders' convention, and Andy Robinson, the convention's main speaker.

Across from the elevators and just outside the lecture room, Andy was involved in an animated discussion with a few men in suits.

The way he moved, gestured, the passion and excitement in his voice, caught Maxwell's attention immediately. Andy actually reminded Maxwell of a character in his novel, the one faithful companion of Sebastian Eldritch, Marvis Cranley, who was a sometimes sidekick, a sometimes court jester, and a full-time spiritual advisor. He started watching Andy because of this fascinating parallel, but then continued watching him because he was such a captivating speaker. When Andy and the two men (who were also listening to him with rapt attention) moved down the hall, Maxwell spotted the poster-board bearing Andy's grin, and a table covered with the man's motivational books.

The phone began to ring, bringing him out of his silent reminiscence. Maxwell turned and regarded the phone, answering machine and key cup on the small table near the front door.

You can only deal with one distraction at a time. Don't let them gang up on you.

He slid the novel back into place on the shelf between THE ARMIES OF DAYLIGHT by Barbara Hambly and FROSTWING by Richard A. Knaak, two of his favourite fantasy authors. The answering machine picked up after the second ring.

"Hi, Sweetie." His mother's voice, slightly tinny coming through the answer machine speaker, filled the hallway. "I'm just worried because I haven't heard from you in a couple of days. Call me." Damn woman, he thought, continuing his journey down the hallway, making him call her twice a week, as if there were anything important to discuss that often. What a waste of time.

Without breaking stride, Maxwell ripped the phone cord out of the wall and carried the unit out the door. In the entranceway, he lifted the lid off the trash can and dropped the phone inside. "I'm busy, Mom," he said as he snuggled the lid back into place. "I'll deal with you later."

Put aside those extra distractions until you have the time to deal with them.

Maxwell then rounded the house. In the front yard, a red-haired kid with a speckling of freckles across his nose stood waving his arms in the air. It was his neighbour's kid, Danny.

"Sorry, Mr. Bronte. I'm so sorry."

Reaching the boy, Maxwell stopped. "Danny, what did I say about throwing the ball against the side of my house?"

Danny didn't answer.

"Danny. What did I say?"

The boy shifted his left foot in front of his right one, softly digging his toe into the grass as he looked up. "You said not to."

"Not to what?"

"Not to throw the ball against the house because it distracts you when you're –"

"That's right," Maxwell said, cutting the child off. "And you disobeyed me. Again."

"I'm sorry, Mr. Bronte. I'm sorry. Can I have my ball back?"

As Maxwell stood there looking at the boy, he was reminded of the fact that this distraction was taking up even more of his time. Andy Robinson's smooth calm voice of reason filled his head. *Distractions are anti-traction. You must give yourself traction by eliminating distraction.*

"Eliminate distraction," Maxwell mumbled. "You want your ball? Here!" He drew his arm back, and with that, the boy immediately stopped sobbing. He started to stumble backwards, his wide eyes never leaving the ball, as Maxwell followed through on his pitch and sent the ball straight at the boy's head.

The ball bounced off the boy's forehead, the shock, more than anything, dropping him to the ground on his backside.

"And stay out of my yard!"

The boy turned, scrambled forward about a foot on his hands and knees, then got to his feet and ran across the yard to the neighbour's house.

After watching the boy run inside and hearing the satisfying slam of the door, Maxwell stood there a moment, taking in a breath of fresh air, carried in on a dry warm desert wind. Then he headed back into the house.

"Oh great," he said, noticing the grass stains on his hand that must have come from the ball. "Running out of time, here."

Andy's voice came to him again. *Time is your friend, not your enemy. Embrace it. Make the most of it.*

He glanced at his watch as he headed toward the bathroom. He only got one day off a week to work on his writing and so far he'd been wasting it with minor distractions. But, as he now knew, *there is no such thing as a minor distraction. Every single distraction is evil and must be dealt with or they will soon stockpile and run your life.* For the past five years, he'd let distractions get in his way. They'd stockpiled in front of him, preventing him from getting anything accomplished. Job Interviews, Funerals, Marriage Counsellors. Distractions with capital letters, all of them, preventing him from getting down to his novel. But not anymore.

Not with the sound words of Andy Robinson to inspire him along.

When Maxwell got to the washroom, he turned on the water, not bothering to wait for the hot water to start coming out. No. That would be a waste of time. He smiled at himself in the mirror as he washed his hands. The new Maxwell smiled back at him.

Say goodbye to the you that says, 'Perhaps I'll do it later.' And say hello to the you that says, 'I want it right now!'

The new Maxwell didn't procrastinate and thought of time as his best friend. Because *time was too powerful to work against.*

Hey, that was a good one he'd just made up on his own.

Not only was Maxwell taking charge of his life, but he was able to rework Andy's strong and powerful words into his own life. After all, it was Andy who said: *Don't just follow these tips blindly. Take them. Use them as your own, and they will evolve into your own words, your own tips, your own maxims.*

Still smiling, Maxwell felt something soft and furry rubbing up against his leg. He looked down at an orange tabby, Smuckers, as it purred and wound back and forth between his legs. Maxwell's smile began to falter as it continued this pattern without pause. And he knew it wouldn't stop until the animal was either fed or petted or perhaps both.

In any case, it was just another distraction.

Still smiling, Maxwell scooped the tabby up, carried it to the toilet and forced its head under the water. Within a couple of minutes the struggling was over, and he set the toilet lid back down, the cat's orange tail still sticking out. He'd been surprised that the feline hadn't put up more of a fight.

Soon, he would have to clean the body out of there. But he couldn't worry about that now. He had to remain focused on the job at hand. *Prioritize your list. What is important? What can wait?*

As he washed his hands, Maxwell became aware of a stinging sensation on his left arm. He turned his wrist over and discovered that the cat must have indeed fought back at least a little. There, on his skin, was a puffed up red scratch. The center of the scratch had opened and a thin line of blood leaked out.

"Not another distraction," Maxwell mumbled, opening up the medicine cabinet. Unable to find any bandages, he stormed out into the hallway.

The doorbell rang.

Maxwell turned towards the door.

On the other side of the screen door stood his neighbour, Gus Sherrington. Gus looked like a much older version of his son, Danny, complete with the thick patch of freckles across his nose. But his red hair had receded to nothing more than a patch of wispy tufts a few inches above each ear. The way he was breathing, in big dramatic gasps, and the look on the man's face suggested that Gus was none too happy that Maxwell had beaned his son with the Indian rubber ball.

Gus raised a baseball bat where Maxwell could see it. "Get yoh ass out heah!" he screamed through the door. "I'll kick yoh ass down the frickin' street for touchin' mah boy."

Distractions have a way of compounding themselves, becoming more than the sum of their parts. "No kidding," Maxwell mumbled, stepping over to the closet. He opened the closet door and reached in for his shotgun.

Eliminating distractions, at any cost, is often your only solution.

"Get yoh ass out heah!" Gus yelled again, unable to see Maxwell checking to ensure the gun was loaded behind the cover of the closet door.

"I said . . ." Gus started to say, but stopped as Maxwell closed the closet door and revealed the gun. Gus's eyes were suddenly as wide as his son's had been when he knew he was going to be getting his ball back the fast and hard way.

Stepping forward and raising the shotgun to chest level, Maxwell fired. The glass and screen shattered in an explosive blast, and Gus was knocked backward off his feet, almost as much from the sound as from the force hitting him in the chest.

Maxwell stepped forward, looking at the man lying on the sidewalk on his back. His eyes wide and terrified, were fixed on

Maxwell; his chest, now hitching even more dramatically than before, was pretty much a stewed up mess of blood, skin, pellets and the remains of his yellow t-shirt. His right hand still clutched the baseball bat and his left hand pawed at the grass, as if it alone could drag him away from further pain.

Distractions are often over before you stop being distracted by them. Could that be the case now? Certainly, Gus wasn't a distraction any longer; he should let him be.

Maxwell turned and headed back down the hallway.

A trickle of blood leaked down his forehead. He figured it must be a cut from the glass, either from the screen door just now or the glass that flew through the air when the ball came through his window.

Whatever it had been, it signalled a need for more bandages.

He stormed towards the master bedroom. "Doris, where are the bandage—"

He paused at the bedroom door. His wife was lying on the floor, her dead hand still clutching the vacuum cleaner wand.

"Oh yeah," Maxwell muttered, remembering. His wife had had the nerve to start vacuuming when she knew he had a lot of work to get done. What a stupid thing to do. He was going to miss her. Strange how quickly he'd forgotten about killing her.

Once you eliminate a distraction, you should forget that it ever existed. Or else it will consume your mind, and your time. That is why distractions are so evil. That is why they must be vanquished.

He decided enough time had been wasted. Without Doris around to help find the bandages, he'd probably never locate them.

Instead, he headed back to his den. He sat in front of the computer, smiled as he propped the shotgun against his desk and lifted his coffee, now cool, to his lips, and relished in the silence of the afternoon.

Now that the distractions were removed, he could get some work done.

After all, there was only so much time to write.

Off in the distance, a wailing siren started to lurk up out of the silence.

Unless it pertains to you directly, ignore anything that threatens to distract you. Deal with it only when it begins to directly interfere with your goal.

Maxwell sent a sideways glance at the shotgun propped up against his desk and then typed, figuring he could at least finish his next paragraph before the police car reached his house.

As he typed, Andy Robinson's smiling face watched him proudly from the cover of the book.

FROM OUT OF THE NIGHT

ALTHOUGH TECHNOLOGY dominates our world today, there still exist things that have been with us since we huddled in caves around brightly burning fires and avoided ominous shadows. Strange beings of the night become frighteningly real to us even now as we venture into the twenty-first century. Unknown things are still out there going bump in the night; a night where most of our dreams are nightmares. Scientifically, we have grown out of the dark ages, but our fears will forever remain among other frightened figures, jumping at shadows outside the cave.

And perhaps for good reason . . .

☠　　　　☠　　　　☠

Mary's screech from the kitchen came to Jack over a simple, old-fashioned baby monitor. "Here they come!"

Jack was in his basement den, putting the finishing touches on another promising non-fiction book about fear and the unknown. On the shelf before him sat several of his more popular published texts: One on Bigfoot, another on the Loch Ness Monster, several on U.F.O.'s, and then the books about a popular television series featuring a pair of FBI paranormal investigators back in the ninety's.

25

Upon hearing Mary's voice he leaned away from the computer, ran his fingers along the base of the keyboard and then turned the screen off. Regretfully nodding to his unfinished project, he got to his feet and headed up the stairs.

Unseen by Mary as he reached the top of the stairs, he stood silently and observed his wife peering out the kitchen window. He studied her familiar features thinking of how often he saw her but didn't really look. Her worn face gave her the impression of someone much older than her forty-three years. She stood over the kitchen counter, silent for a moment. Her expression told him her mind was racing furiously.

When their teenaged son entered the room, Mary's head swung to orient on him, her face displaying a queer blank.

He gazed curiously at his mother.

"John, the lights!"

John clicked the kitchen light off in haste. He then moved to the front door and locked it." Are they back again, Mom?"

Mary gazed proudly at her son as he locked the door. "Smart move. And yes, they're back." She twisted to look out the window again. "There go a few of them now, to Mrs. Hancock's house. Oh, and there's another two coming up the other side of the street. Oh!" She ducked. "I don't think they saw me!"

"Why are there so many of them this time, Mom?"

"Because they're growing in strength and in number. They feed on our fear and prey on the weak-minded. They coerce others into becoming just like them. And they won't be satisfied until everyone is a blood-thirsty, flesh-eating demon like they are. They won't stop until everyone has Become."

A burst of laughter filled the room and Mary jumped, swinging her head in the direction of the living room. A smile of relief crossed her face and Jack could tell, even before she spoke, that it had only been the canned laughter of a television sitcom audience.

"Susie!" Mary shrieked. "Turn off that TV!"

The television continued to play. Another wave of laughter from the studio audience flooded the darkened room.

Mary turned to face her son, a barely controlled panic in her eyes. "Listen, John. Take your sister and go down to the basement. Tell your father to shut off his den lights and you hide with him there.

I don't want those cannibals to get anywhere near you two. Do you hear me?"

As Jack watched them, a wave of nostalgia overcame him. It was so obvious her only concern was for her children. She was willing to sacrifice herself for them without a second thought. It made Jack pine for the days when their own love had been so unselfish. But that had been years ago, before their relationship had evolved into something more mature, something increasingly less demonstrative. It was nothing like his active love for his writing. It was simply there.

While John went into the living room to get his little sister, Jack moved silently into the kitchen. His eyes met Mary's as the light and noise of the television stopped. In a thickened darkness they looked at each other and listened to their children stumble to the stairway.

"I love you," Mary whispered at their sounds in the dark. When they were gone she addressed her husband. "The kids'll be safer down there, hidden away. They won't have access to them."

"Why don't you go downstairs with the kids, hon?" Jack suggested. "Let me handle them tonight."

"No. I'm not defenceless. I can protect my family just fine. Now get yourself back downstairs and look after my children. They're going to need someone with them."

"Mary, please," he said, reaching out to touch her shoulder. "I can protect us."

Flinching back from his touch, Mary glared at him. "No. No, you can't. If you'd wanted to protect us you would have put the boards up like I suggested."

"We don't need the boards, Mary." Jack thought back to the year before when she'd insisted that he nail boards on all the windows and doors. They'd stayed in the boarded up house for three days. Fortunately, the kids were able to get an online hook up to their classrooms so they didn't miss school. And Jack's writing work hardly had him leaving the basement den, never mind the house. So it hadn't been that much of a hardship. But he couldn't justify using the boards this year. The nuisance was just too much this time. His manuscript was already overdue and his agent was calling three times a day; twice less than his editor.

"Yes, we do need the boards. The boards were probably the only thing that saved us last time." She crossed her arms and paced the length of the kitchen, careful to stay out of touching distance. "What about Mr. and Mrs. Allen two doors down? They didn't board up their house last year and look what's happened to them. They're changing, they're *Becoming*. They may not be consuming flesh yet, but you can tell they've started to change. You can see it in their eyes. *Becoming* doesn't happen overnight, Jack. It has to grow and fester inside them over time. It's a horrible process of self-induced pain and suffering."

"Mary, I honestly don't think it was because of the boards. We'll be perfectly safe without them."

"You're right, the Allens were weak. Ted and Lisa just couldn't resist their supernatural charms and promises of immortality. But they wouldn't have had to resist them had they boarded themselves up inside." She peeked out the window once more. "Oh damn! We forgot to turn off the outside porch light. Quick, get the switch. Get the switch!"

Jack reached for the light switch.

"Too late!" she cried. "Too damn late! A group of them have already spotted the light. They're drawn to it like moths, Jack. Like sick, disgusting insects." She swallowed noisily and ran a hand down the side of her face. "Looks like I'm going to have to finally face them. Well, at least you and the kids will be safely hidden."

Jack stepped forward, feeling guilty. He couldn't even remember the words of comfort he used to be able to find for her when she'd needed his strength. Despite the urgency of the situation, the desperation in her voice, his mind kept wandering back to his unfinished manuscript. No matter how hard he tried, he honestly wanted nothing more than to go downstairs and continue writing.

Feeling like a poseur, he tried again. "Mary please. Go downstairs and let me handle it."

"No. You don't know all their tricks, Jack. They have to be invited in. They can only corrupt those who invite them in. There's no need for all of us to be exposed to their horrors. Besides, I'm the strongest minded. Maybe they won't be able to convert me into one of them. I should be strong enough to resist them."

"You're right," Jack sighed. She was right, too. She was one stubborn lady, impossible to sway once her mind was set. He knew that all too well. "I know you can do it. I'll go downstairs and wait with the kids. Good luck, Mary." He headed for the basement stairs.

"Wait, Jack. Before you go, promise me something."

He paused on the top step.

"It would kill me to corrupt my own family, but that's what they do, that's how they survive, isn't it? By making others like them? Promise me that if, after this meeting with them tonight, if I Become, you'll take the children far away from me. Promise me you'll do everything you can to prevent the kids from *Becoming*. Promise me that."

Jack took a deep breath. "I promise."

A heavy knock sounded through the darkness. "This is it." She leaned back against the counter and sighed. "I'll wait a minute and make sure you're safely hidden. I love you."

A tear came to Jack's eye. He brushed it away. "I love you too, Mary." The words rolled off his tongue like a forgotten language. He quickly moved down the stairs.

When Jack got to the den, he closed the door behind him and sat in the armchair near the computer. Susie ran over to him, jumped into his lap, and threw her arms around him. She was trembling.

Over the baby monitor, he could hear Mary's footsteps upstairs as she moved to open the door. Turning the monitor off, he frowned in an attempt to suppress a chuckle. "It's all right, Susie. It's okay. Mommy's going to be okay."

She looked at him questioningly and found courage in her father's eyes and voice. Jack was slightly irritated at how Mary's behaviour had frightened their daughter. John understood what was wrong with his mother, but Susie, being four, was still too young to make sense of it. All she knew was that mommy was scared to death of those *Christians.*

The Christians, with their non-scientific belief in life after death, resurrection of the dead, and their weekly consumption of another man's flesh and blood.

Mary was a perfect wife and mother in all other respects; so what was so wrong in having one paranoid delusion? It was natural. In fact, Jack based his living on other people's paranoid delusions and fears. Paranoia and fear helped to feed his family. And besides, it was a simple harmless paranoia. *It's not like Mary would ever hurt anybody.*

Suddenly inspired, Jack put his daughter down and told the children to watch the television in the room across the hall so long as they kept the door closed and the volume low.

He brought his hands down gently on the keyboard, and, smiling, he wrote what he felt would be a satisfying conclusion to the introductory chapter.

☠   ☠   ☠

Irritation occurs in the believer's heart when science or the reason of daylight find rational ways of knocking their beliefs and fears. But given the fact that proving the non-existence of anything is virtually impossible, fears continue to haunt us. We are pursued from out of the night by dreams of the unknown and visions of the unexplainable – the unreal. Even if, one day, proof is given that our fear-created beings do not actually exist, we will probably invent new ones.

☠   ☠   ☠

The doorway to the den opened, startling Jack out of his reverent typing. He looked up as Mary's throaty laugh filled the room. "I did it, Jack," she said. "I protected my family from them. They're never going to get us now."

Mary stood in the doorway clutching a blood stained butcher knife and smiled a bright white-toothed grin at him from beneath a coat of deep crimson.

He looked at her a moment and realised the frightening truth. There were no more monsters out there. Ghosts, vampires, witches and bogeymen had all been vanquished. Monsters, creatures of the night and ghouls had all been conquered, and there was no need to create new ones. The only monsters left were the ones inside our own hearts. The demon thoughts that allowed Mary to obsess over something she was afraid of until the insanity finally consumed her; the spirits of selfishness that allowed Jack to simply overlook her problems because he was too busy focussing on himself and his writing. These personal monsters people never want to face, were the only nightmares left.

These thoughts, his most brilliant conclusion yet, would never make it to the printed page, because for the first time in eight years, Jack completely forgot about his writing as he got up, went over to his wife and held her while she wept.

CURT CRIES IN THE NIGHT

Short short stories and poetry

☠

NERVOUS TWITCHING

THE NIGHT was cold and the air murky. Samantha's blood was dark and still warm as it poured out onto the cool pavement from beneath her shoulder blades.

Neil Hunter was afraid.

Sort of.

He couldn't quite remember what had happened . . . *here, it's heavy. It takes two hands just to lift it* . . . but the results were plainly obvious. Samantha was now dead.

Sort of.

Relax. Hold it down. Expose the neck. That's it. Good, Neil. Good boy.

Samantha's head rested on the alley floor about two feet away from her body. Burning tears welled in Neil's eyes. What had happened to her? And why couldn't he remember it?

Well he *could* remember it.

Sort of.

Good, son. Don't lose your grip. Lift the axe, aim and drop. Quickly.

He remembered seeing her head rolling away from her body. And hearing the echoes of her screams bouncing off the alley walls.

Something else echoed there, too. Laughter?

Look at them fluttering helplessly about the yard. It's funny, but not funny. It's somehow pitiful. And the worst thing is that I can't help but watch and laugh.

Neil bowed over and released the contents of his stomach onto the cool pavement, beside the fresh crimson liquid pooling on the alley floor.

Steam slowly rose from the pair of liquids.

Beside him, her headless body twitched.

He looked up at the decapitated head through the blur of tears.

"Help me," her lips seemed to say as her mouth moved.

Dad. They won't stop running around. Do they even know they're dead?

And her eyes. They were vacant and staring.

Sort of.

For sometimes her eyes seemed to move, seemed to be following his own movements.

It's nervous twitching, Neil. They'll stop. Funny how they flutter about even after they are dead, isn't it? But we both know that it's really just nervous twitching. Nothing more.

Neil knelt by Samantha's head, the taste of bile still strong in his throat. Although his stomach continued to churn and his heart continued to ache, he could no longer throw up or cry.

He was beyond all that.

Sort of.

Nothing more than nervous twitching. Keep watching son. They'll stop.

Shivering in the cool night air, he picked up her head, the left cheek matted with blood, now cold, and cradled it in his arms.

He could feel her lips working against his chest.

Sort of funny how they twitch. But they're not stopping, Dad. They're not stopping!

THE BOGEYMAN CAN

"Who can take a garbage bag?
– (garbage bag) –
And stuff it full of kids?
– (stuff it full of kids) –
Who can kill anyone he wants to?
And get away with it?

(The Bogeyman)

The Bogeyman can
Cause he stays right out of sight
Until the lights go down . . ."

"OKAY, HOLD it! Stop the film! Lights!"
"What? What's wrong now, Martin?"
The lights in the mini theatre came on.
Martin massaged the top of his shiny, round head, sucking the last half inch left of his cigarette. He sighed as he flicked the butt into his companion's coffee where it fizzled, unnoticed by Rogers.

"I give you two extra weeks and half a million dollars and you come up with this crap? You come up with a mockery — and a poor one at that — of the Candyman song?"

Rogers stared at Martin with thin red eyes. He had spent the last seventy hours attempting to complete the "Bogeyman" music video on time. And he'd just made it. The money this lousy assignment would earn him would help pay for the studio space he needed to cut his first record. He'd planned on going home and dropping into a very deep sleep until the secretary told him he was supposed to stay with Mr. Martin for the screening of the video.

Great.

If there was one thing he didn't feel like doing, it was sitting beside the old fart in the mini theatre and listening to the whistling noise he made while he breathed. All that Rogers had wanted was to drop off the film, pick up his cheque and never have to see Martin's ugly mug again. But, as he should have suspected, Martin was not easily satisfied. The video had barely begun to run when Martin screamed for it to stop.

"This product has been ready to go for a week now, but we didn't release it. They tell me it's time, but I say 'Hold on fellows: I've got the best man in the business working on our promotional video. He's young and new, but I know he'll deliver. Give him another week. Rogers won't let us down!' Well, Rogers, you've made a lying bastard out of me!" Martin's dome began blushing as he ranted.

"Look, man!" Rogers paused, trying to pull his words together. "It's a rock video. You barely let the video begin. If you'd give it half a chance . . ."

"Half a chance? Rogers, this song makes a laughing stock out of the 'Bogeyman' line. It's supposed to be a serious product with advertisements aimed at the parents. Your stupid lyrics belittle the importance — the current social need — of the product. They make fun of it. And you aimed the damn thing at the kids."

"It's a kids toy." Rogers was barely aware of the words he was uttering. He had enough trouble keeping his eyes open, never mind trying to keep up with the blithering bald man stewing in front of him.

"But no kid in their right mind would buy the thing. It's a product which parents will be buying for their kids." Martin got up, walked over to the nearest wall, slammed his fist into it and then sat back down again. "Rogers, look at me. Look at me! Did you even bother to read the marketing package I gave to you?"

"Package?"

"The description of our product and of our target market, you idiot."

Rogers leaned forward and sipped his coffee. There was a weird taste to it. It was cold. No, that wasn't it. There was something else. He looked down into his cup at the floating cigarette butt.

"Did you read the package?"

"I never got the bloody package!' Anger gave him his second wind — or was it his third, fourth or fifth wind? Who knew? Being awake this many hours made it hard to think. "Besides, what's there to know? It's a product called 'The Bogeyman.' It scares little kids into being good. I left spaces in the video for your marketing editor to insert stills of the thing. What the hell else do you want from me?"

"*Stills of the thing*? *Stills of the thing*? You stupid fool. You think by adding still photos of our 'Bogeyman' overtop of your pathetic, childish jingle, anyone would ever buy our product? Do you even understand how much time and resources you've wasted?"

Martin walked over to the wall where he had slammed his fist. He signaled the technician in the projection booth. The opposite wall opened up with an annoying squeal.

Rogers rubbed his eyes and tried to look into the darkened corridor beyond the wall, but he couldn't see in. Dammit, something stunk to high hell. Was it him? He sniffed at his armpits.

The echoes of a soft moving — slithering — came from the corridor. A mist rolled out and settled across the floor of the mini theatre. It was the mist that stunk. Rogers felt a chill and sipped the coffee once more. Oh shit! He'd forgotten the stupid cigarette butt.

"What the hell's goin' on, man?"

The dark silhouette of a tall skinny shape appeared in the entrance of the corridor. Rogers couldn't make out any features through the mist which curled around the figure like a dark robe.

Martin waved a boney finger in Rogers' direction, shaking his head. "He's been a bad boy. A very bad boy." He spun on his heels and headed for the door.

"Martin. Where are you going?"

"To get another song writer. A good one." Martin called to the production booth as he stepped out of the room, quickly closing the door behind him. "Lights!" The slamming of the door was instantly followed by the sound of the door being locked.

The lights dipped, plunging the room into darkness. Even the exit signs at the top of the house and the work lights from the projection booth went out. The foul smell intensified with the encroaching darkness. Rogers heard the slithering sound again. It too, was louder, closer.

Through the door he thought he could hear Martin's voice, somewhat calmer; somewhat more satisfied. "You know, some of those lyrics you wrote might be useful after all: *The Bogeyman can, cause he stays right out of sight until the lights go down.*"

A noise very much like a cross between a screech and a growl echoed through the darkness as something slimy and large picked Rogers up by the top of his head.

The howling groan of the creature reminded him of Martin's laughter.

ALMOST

THE DARK woods were far from still. A strong wind made the tops of the trees bow. A low howl accompanied the wind as it forced its way around the branches and through the leaves. Orange and yellow corpses fluttered from the trees to the ground, never to be buried, merely trampled upon.

Muffled by the call of the wind, Dale Garrison crunched upon the newly fallen leaves as he ran through the forest. He stumbled to a tree and leaned against it, listening, watching.

Out of breath, he looked back over his shoulder. He'd gotten this far without them picking up his trail. But he couldn't rest long. The dogs would soon pick up his scent and they'd be on his tail again.

The horrid cost of freedom these days, Dale thought, running his left hand across his sweaty brow. He couldn't run like this all night. He'd have to find a ride or something, get out of his Sunnyside Institution uniform and flee the state before word of his escape got out.

It had been twenty minutes since he'd been free. No doubt the local stations had broadcast his escape by now. He had to be very careful. He was an easily identifiable suspect.

The wind howled louder, and he thought that he could pick out the sounds of barking in the distance.

Still out of breath, Dale stumbled forward and broke into a lurching run. A sharp pain stabbed through his side and he tried to ignore it. The tempting smell of freedom, like a carrot held before a starving horse, guided him onward.

Just when he thought he could bear the pain no longer, Dale staggered to a clearing. And before him he found exactly what he needed.

A pale grey Chevrolet was parked in the clearing on a hill overlooking a spectacular view of the town below. Dale could detect two figures inside the car through the steamy windows.

He slowly approached the car, crouching and trying to keep his breathing quiet. He hadn't yet figured out how he would overpower the people inside, as tired as he was, but he knew that he didn't have much time.

Nearing the driver's door, he remained low and peered in through the window. A glance at them would tell him if they would be much of a threat to his freedom.

Things hadn't changed much, Dale thought as he regarded a couple of teenagers making out. The male, thin and short, had his face pressed up against a blond haired female's face. Her hands danced up and down his back to the sound of a pop song on the radio. The male's hands deftly worked at unbuttoning the female's blouse.

The car had been idling. Dale could see the keys in the ignition.

Conflicting thoughts ran through Dale's mind. He wanted to continue watching. The sudden excitement of adolescent sex brought him memories of his own youth. It had been almost a decade since he saw real live breasts. But he needed to get the teens out of the car so that he could escape.

As Dale watched, feeling a stirring in his groin, he calculated his next move. Just as the boy had the girl's blouse open and cupped her breasts between his hands, the muffled voice of the radio announcer interrupted the song.

Dale moved to the back of the car, his plan already formed. All that he had to do was open the passenger door, pull the girl from the car and threaten to kill her if the boy didn't get out. He could then slip into the car and speed away.

From the woods came the distinct sound of barking.

They were getting closer.

Dale moved quickly around the back of the car, and in his haste tripped over something. He landed on his left hand and it twisted beneath him. He let out a yelp.

From within the car, the girl screamed.

Shit, Dale thought, cradling his left arm to his chest. The barking dogs were louder as they echoed in through the trees. As Dale slid forward on his left side, he could hear the boy and girl arguing within the car.

By the time he reached the passenger door, the arguing seemed to be over. As Dale reached forward and grasped the door handle with his right hand, the car started moving.

Searing pain shot through Dale's right arm as the car peeled away. He cradled the bloody stump at the end of his right arm to his chest and watched the car peel away down the dirt road, heading back to town.

Goddamn cheap doctors at the institution, Dale thought, listening as the barking dogs neared the edge of the clearing. They had the technology to provide him with a workable plastic right hand after the accident at the prison shop. But he was a criminal.

He moaned as he lay on the ground, the exhaust and dust from the car settling on his face. The dogs burst through the trees, the excited shouts of the cops not far behind.

They had the technology, but wouldn't waste it – or the money, for that matter – on a criminal slated for death row. Goddamn cheap doctors.

He almost had gotten away. He would have been able to open the door in time, if not for that useless prosthetic hand. As the first dog reached him, he vaguely wondered when they would discover the hook stuck in the door handle.

THE SOUND OF ONE MAN SCREAMING

A pen is lifted from a cup
          that waits, patiently, on the edge of the desk
Sometimes in haste
Sometimes with measured care
The pen is lifted, balanced between three fingers
          and brought down to kiss an empty page

A blank computer screen glares
The incessant whirring of a hard-drive fan
          an undying, steady rhythmic pulse
Both mocking the absence of activity in the room
Until the distinct sound of fingers clacking the keyboard
          announce the presence of words on the screen

A coffee mug filled with a simple black blend
Sometimes full
Sometimes cool
Often touched merely for the comfort it offers
          overlooks the entire process

If you listen very carefully you will hear
More silent than the sound of the steam rising off the coffee
Ever so gently
The sound of one man screaming

FROST AFTER MIDNIGHT

The Frost performs its secret ministry
While I perform my own. My victim's cries
Come loud – and hark, again – but then no more
The inmates of the cottage, all at rest,
Leaving me to a solitude which sutis
My morbid musings: glance down at my side
In death my infant slumbers peacefully

WITH APOLOGIES TO E.P.

Are you vengeful tonight?
Will you come back tonight?
Are you pissed 'cause I sliced you
apart?
Does your undead mind stray
To that bright summer day
When I killed you and carved out your heart?

Are the chairs in your parlour
Still bloodied and stained?
Have you crawled from your grave site
To haunt me again?

Now my heart's filled with fear
For these sounds which I hear
Make me think that
You've come back tonight

THERE IS A LOW AND FEARFUL CRY

There is a low and fearful cry
Which, on occasion, I do hear
When I find myself alone
And prone to silent fear

It stops me in a morbid pose
And brings out thoughts forbidden
Which my conscious mind had tucked away –
Had all but safely hidden

The call is deep and curdles blood
Stirs emotions which I thought were gone
Trembling, I cannot help but
Dance to its unholy song

But when I hear this horrid cry
The dreadful thing I always find
Is that despite its foreign sound
That fearful cry is mine

BLOOD DREAMS

Blood dreams return to me
In the cold dark shroud of sleep
I am prey to their savage hunt each night
The chase always ends
With tepid thick fluid covering me
       drowning me hold me
       helpless
       covering me, drowning me holding me
       keeping me
Covered in blood dreams

Still these blood dreams are a comforting blanket
And the guilt will eventually fade
Or else I'll cease to feel it
In my obsessed and infected mind
But you – you will always be dead
And all because of me
Yes you – you will always be dead
You, the spawn of these blood dreams

WAILIN' JENNY

Mama, don't let your babies grow up to be cowboys
(She sings)
Mama don't let your little ones grow up at all –
'Cause they're better to eat
Once you chop off their feet
And, preserved, they can last through next fall

HOLIDAY DEMONS

Drifting down the street, demons
Masquerade as children who in turn
Are dressed in flame-retardant costumes
But they don't fool me
They never have

Ghosts and goblins giggling, plotting
Their devilish little minds whirling
As they huddle together across the lane
Discussing their plan of attack
For the night

Motionless, maniacal rubber grins
Hide the true horror which I know lurks
Beneath their masks
As they turn to see me
Watching them

I know too much – I always have

Clutching the knife, I await their
Supposedly innocent approach
I'll kill them the way I killed that fat guy
Who snuck in through my fireplace last winter

THE SOUND OF CLAPPING

Stories that have been nominated for awards or given special mention

☠

PHANTOM MITCH

EVEN THOUGH he no longer had his left arm, Barry could still feel an itch between the thumb and index finger of his non-existent left hand. I believe they call it the phantom itch.

But that was only the beginning.

Sometimes Barry would lie in bed, still half asleep, and feel a hand take his phantom left one and hold it reassuringly. He'd sit up and sense some sort of presence in the room with him, but the feeling would quickly fade. That, more than the itch, was making him crazy. If only he could touch her back.

Her? Did I say her? Then I'd better explain.

The presence Barry felt was that of his recently departed wife, Michelle — known as Mitch to Barry and close friends, like me. He was sure it was her. And if I was willing to believe that he experienced a phantom itch as well as some sort of phantom hand touching his, why shouldn't I believe that he somehow knew it was the phantom hand of his dead wife?

I'd been distressed when news of Barry's accident came. It hadn't come as a shock, though. Despite his generosity and his friendly manner, he'd had a problem with alcohol. Barry liked his job and loved his wife; but he cherished his scotch.

Barry had been drinking, as usual, and driving.

He'd left the party a happy drunk, as was typical for him. Even though he drank excessively on social occasions he still retained a pleasant disposition. Perhaps that was why we never actively encouraged him to seek help. He wasn't an annoying drunk. Nor did his problem seem to impinge on his life. He had still continued to lead a successful career, keep his loving wife and maintain active social relationships.

No, his drinking hadn't been a problem. It hadn't been, until that night when he left the party a happy drunk and ended up at the bottom of a canyon, pinned inside a twisted steel hulk which used to be his Cadillac.

The loss he'd experienced from the accident was tragic. Not only had he lost his left eye, his entire left arm and the ability to move his legs, but he also lost his wife.

"It's Mitch, you know." Barry said to me one day as I sat beside his bed. "I can tell that it's her hand holding mine. You know how? There was a scar on her palm, about an inch long, where she'd sliced it open on a broken pane of glass in her grandfather's barn when she was twelve. And when that phantom hand touches mine, I can feel that scar and I know it's her.

"Each time she holds my hand, it lasts longer; and it's beginning to feel more physical, more solid. It's as if I'm starting to really connect with Mitch. Because now I'm able to squeeze back. Yeah, slowly I'm learning how to move and control my phantom hand.

"And sometimes I think that she's trying to talk to me. But I can't hear her, because I still have both my ears, you know. It's like I can only sense her with my hand because I don't have it anymore."

By that time I'd considered giving up on Barry. Okay, experiencing a phantom itch was easy to believe; so was holding the phantom hand of his dead wife. In a sense it was a touching, romantic notion. A tasty morsel for the mind to snack on. But to actually believe that somehow Mitch was in a phantom world parallel to our own, trying to communicate with him, well that was a tougher bit of meat to chew, never mind swallow.

Despite my hesitation to believe, I didn't give up on Barry. I still visited him at least once a week. I had been the best man at his wedding, and for years his closest friend. I know he'd have done the same for me had I been in his position, so I couldn't let him down.

The next time I saw him, he updated me on his phantom encounters with Mitch.

"I felt her breasts," Barry smiled up at the ceiling as he relayed the events of the night before. "It started off with the usual thing, you know. I could feel her hand touching mine, and I squeezed back.

"But then her hand slipped out of mine. I thought that she was gone again, when I felt a soft mound of flesh — her bare breast — in my palm. My thumb rolled across the nipple and I felt it respond to my touch. She shifted and let me feel the other one. I began to cry. God, it had been so long since I touched her."

His encounters — or his hallucinations, or whatever you want to call them — were beginning to get more vivid, and with that, more erotic. He'd describe them to me as soon as I arrived. And after a while, it was the only thing we talked about.

Okay, so I had trouble believing some of the things he said. But his stories intrigued me, and soon enough I was visiting him every single day. He'd progressed from feeling her breasts to other sexual activities. After a while, they'd done everything a man and woman could do together with the one appendage he had available in that phantom world.

She'd let him caress her entire body except for her face, he told me. She had never been an oral woman anyway, he'd said, so he didn't particularly miss the feel of her lips. And, for as long as I'd known him, Barry had never been turned on by a woman's hair. And Mitch had known that. So, she'd offered up her body instead, letting him explore what she always knew he was interested in.

Then, one day, Barry said it.

"I wish I could make love to her."

And I knew what that meant.

"If I tried to do it myself I'd probably pass out before I could finish," he said, trying to win me over with brutal logic. "So, will you do it for me?"

I refused. I couldn't dismember my friend. It was tough enough just trying to imagine taking a blade and hacking off his penis. It was a ludicrous idea. How would I explain it to the nurses? I pictured myself standing over the bed with Barry's severed penis in my hand and blood spurting from his body. A nurse walks in and I politely ask her the best way to stop the bleeding. I don't think so.

The next few times I visited him after that, we argued about it. But after a while, he seemed to give up on the idea and went back to describing his latest encounter with Mitch.

And soon enough, more interesting things developed.

"If I close my right eye," Barry said. "I can just barely make out her shape using the phantom sight of my left one. It's very fuzzy:

unclear. But it's getting better every time. Every night when she returns, her image comes into focus just a little bit more. It's like the hand. The more I use it, the better it gets. Pretty soon I'll be able to see her."

I left the hospital that day, excited with the idea that soon he'd have another sensory input into this phantom world. I know, I know. I had started off a nonbeliever; but when you think about the possibilities of what Barry claimed he could do, doesn't it make you stop and think? Maybe this is proof of an existence beyond death. And if there is, did Barry discover a way for the living to reach into it?

I wanted to tell someone. But who would believe it?

I also briefly considered removing one of my own hands to see what I could discover for myself in this phantom plane; but it was only a momentary thought and on a level far removed from possibility. I'd look at the axe, then at my wrist, and somewhere, tucked away deep in my mind, I could imagine myself reaching for it.

Anyway, I couldn't tell anyone. And I didn't have the guts — or the stupidity; it depends on how you look at it — to try it myself. So I'd have to go on exploring this new world through Barry, and hope that would be enough.

And it was enough. Until yesterday.

Apparently, Barry had killed himself during the night. It was a quiet, peaceful death, they said. He'd overdosed on a handful of painkillers which he must have ben saving up for weeks. Had he been saving them so he could go through with his plans of dismemberment? I often wondered about that.

I was given a box of his personal items, since he had no family and I was his closest friend. I returned home, filled a tall glass with Glenfiddich and drank in memory of Barry as I gazed through what was left of his life.

A hair brush, a photo of Barry & Mitch — taken at the Grand Canyon, I think — a toothbrush, a pack of well worn playing cards with rounded edges.

Then I discovered a sealed envelope with my name on it. I opened it and removed a single sheet of paper. It was dated the night he had died.

Goodbye, my friend, it read. *Thank you for sticking around, for listening to me. But I'd like to thank you especially for refusing my idiotic request. I don't think I'd have been able to hold out this long — long enough to write this letter to you — if I'd gone through with it.*

I saw Mitch tonight. Finally. But it wasn't what I'd hoped it would be.

I can't describe the burning in my heart when I saw what had become of her. I know that there's an existence beyond ours, because I've touched a part of it. But I didn't know that when you die you carry over certain things: things pertaining to your death.

I'd yearned for so long to see her again. And when I finally did I just couldn't deal with it. I'm hoping that passing completely into death — completely into Mitch's world — will make me better able to handle this. Maybe then I wouldn't care anymore. Maybe then I could make love to her without this feeling of dread.

Maybe in death I'll be more accepting.

So, goodbye, my friend. Wish me luck.

I crumpled the letter and downed the scotch in one gulp. Then I refilled the glass to do it again, but my stomach heaved and I had to run to the toilet.

The cold, wet porcelain felt good as I knelt there, staring at nothing, the bitter scent and taste of bile strong in my nostrils and on my tongue.

I find myself returning to that stance whenever I think about it.

Barry said that you carried certain things into the other world with you. Things pertaining to your death. There was only one thing he could have meant by that.

In the accident, Mitch had been beheaded.

ERRATIC CYCLES

CHARLES DEAN Webster, attorney at law, sat very still in his '89 Toyota Tercel, frustrated over his predicament. Something — he had no idea what — had happened to his car. First there had been smoking and hissing and then the car had stopped running. That was the extent of his knowledge about what was wrong with his car. He was a lawyer, not a mechanic.

Dammit Jim, I'm a lawyer, not a mechanic.

He looked at his watch, taking his eyes off of the forest for only a very short time. It was a quarter past nine. As he lifted his head to look down the barren stretch of Highway 144, he caught the glare of the setting sun in his rearview mirror.

"Damn!"

He slammed a fist against the dash and then sat back once more and stared out the bug splattered windshield at the deserted highway.

Why me? he asked, and was quick to find an answer.

Why not you?

This was going to be your big case, your first major success, your big break. This was going to be the case that not only brought you a handsome sum but spread your name across the country. After winning this one, you were finally going to be someone.

So why not you? If you continue to believe such stupid glorified dreams, then why not you? Face the facts, schmuck: This is just another case.

And, being just another case, it had been nothing but a pain in the ass from day one. Getting stranded on a lonely highway somewhere between Sudbury and Timmins was just par for the course.

He looked at his watch again, but only a minute had passed since he'd last checked it. His eyes quickly returned to the wall of forest which ran never-ending along both sides of the highway. He couldn't shake the feeling that something was watching him from the forest.

No, not *something*, he corrected himself.

The Bush People.

He shuddered at that thought and considered turning on the radio to help alleviate his mood; but he was afraid that it would kill the battery. And he needed the battery in order for the hazard lights to keep working? Didn't he?

Dammit, it always came back to that, didn't it?

He hated the fact that he knew nothing much about how a car worked. But that had been his father's profession, not his.

When he was still young — very young — he'd watched his father closely. Anthony Webster would come home from the garage and spend as long as twenty minutes washing his hands and never really getting them clean. The tracks of his fingerprints were a permanent resting place for the grease and oil of his livelihood. Then, after supper, he would sit down in the living room with a beer in one hand and a remote in the other and grumble about inflation, taxes and the latest antics of the Toronto Maple Leafs. And the next day the cycle would repeat: *Work, a vain attempt to wash away the residue of that work, and when that failed, a cleansing of the soul with beer and bitching.*

Charles loved and respected his father who had never been anything but reliable and supportive. He'd always provided his only son with everything he could afford to give him and only once had he raised a hand to him — but in retrospect, Charles had deserved that quick slap after having verbally assaulted his mother in a typical teenager/mother argument. Anthony Webster was as close to the perfect father as any man could be.

But the last thing that Charles wanted was to be like him. He could never lead such a mundane existence. Charles wanted more than just money and a career. He wanted an exciting and fulfilling lifestyle. He didn't want his father's life of broken car after broken car — every day slaving over someone else's troubles and ultimately getting nowhere in life.

No, that wasn't for Charles. That wasn't what he wanted at all. He yearned to be a lawyer, to experience the lifestyle portrayed in the *L.A. Law* television series he'd loved so much; so he reached for it.

But he never got it.

Every case he took on held the promise of being *the* case which would move him up. But they never did. Instead, he slaved day after day over someone else's troubles, someone else's broken life, never moving up.

He ended up living the very lifestyle he had dreaded: His father's. Only, Charles lacked many of the things that his father had, including the knowledge of how a car worked.

Charles had been too engrossed in his own personal dreams to bother hanging around with his father and learning a few essential details about his trade.

And because of it, he was stranded.

Caught in the very trap he had attempted to avoid.

So it always did come down to that, didn't it? Running away from something only brought it down on you even worse.

His cellular phone was rendered useless by the remote location he was stranded in. He didn't even know how far it was to the next town, or at least to the next pay phone. If he knew, he might consider walking. It would be far better than sitting around waiting for another car to drive by.

Although it had only been fifteen minutes since he saw any traffic he was afraid that no one else would drive by. He'd never driven out of the concrete corridor before and had no idea of what to expect. Besides, even if someone stopped, would they even bother helping him if they knew who he was?

If only he could get to a phone and make one toll free call to the CAA.

Charles smirked and looked at his watch again without reading it. With <u>his</u> luck, his CAA membership would probably have run out, or for some stupid reason they didn't cover this area. Or perhaps the nearby CAA was run by one of the local groups that despised him. Wouldn't that be a cute confrontation? He wouldn't be surprised if any of these things happened — everything else had gone wrong so far.

It had started out as a simple case. His client, a Toronto-based company called Durban Lumber, had purchased a large chunk of land near Timmins for their logging operations. The only issue when Charles had picked up the case was a local band of Indians claiming traditional rights to the land. But Durban Lumber had purchased the land from the municipality and held legal ownership. It was a straightforward matter of Charles walking in, going through the motions, flashing the ownership papers, quoting a sample of similar past cases in which the defendant was triumphant, and hopefully settling it out of court.

Then a new development changed things. The native lawyers uncovered an old weathered copy of a document that the municipality had signed with the native leaders, recognizing the land as traditionally belonging to them. Because of a fire over two decades earlier at city hall, the municipality's copy of that document had been destroyed and forgotten.

And so the simple case had turned ugly. Durban Lumber was pressing the municipality from one side while the Indians were pressing them from another. The media had eaten the story up, of course, in the popular story of big business stepping all over the little guy.

The more sour the case turned, the more difficult it was for Charles to obtain the upper hand. The stress mounted, the tension increased and it began to get more than sour, more than ugly.

On his last visit to Timmins, a group of environmentalists and Indians greeted his plane at the airport with catcalls, rotten fruit and stones. Charles, the representative of the big bully, became the object of their hatred and anger. They all wanted a piece of him.

Things got so bad that instead of flying in to his next meeting in Timmins, Charles opted to drive. Not only would he arrive in an unexpected manner and hopefully undetected, but he could use the six or so hours that it would take him to get there to relax and sort things out.

It would be the first time he was alone in over seven years. Truly alone — without work and booze, his longtime companions.

After finishing a gruelling law school program, Charles launched straight into his career. He started at the bottom, as most

56

lawyers do, and had remained there ever since. He never once attributed his dire position to burn-out, but instead kept driving himself harder and harder, waiting for that <u>one</u> case.

At least in school when he botched a test or flunked a paper he had the chance of redeeming himself with another test or another paper before the final grades came out. But his career, he discovered, didn't work that way. Mistakes stayed on his record, without the possibility of being wiped out by future successes. There was no chance for redemption — there was only one thing. Plugging on.

So Charles had jumped from a life of study, work, party, sleep, to a life of work, research and more work. There were no study weeks or spring breaks where one could relax and then use the time to catch up on all the areas one had fallen behind in. There were no getaway weekends like there had been in school.

This was a career. This was life. This was not at all what Charles had expected or hoped for.

The only way he could cope was using a method he had learned by watching his father. He coped with the Webster method of bitching and booze. That soon became part of his daily ritual.

Years ago he had lived for the weekends and the promises that once school was finished he would be able to get on with living, with life, with being a free man in a free world. It wasn't long before he discovered that there was no such thing as freedom. There was no such thing as just living.

The barrage of cliches which his father spewed forth daily about the shit that life dealt an honest man were all coming true. Charles found himself not only repeating those same old tired clichés about life, but actually believing them.

Charles had discovered one night in the midst of an alcoholic haze that the cycle his life had taken was no better than his father's. Work like a bastard, the come home and drink like one. Only, his father also had a wife and a son. All that Charles had was work and booze.

It had become time to re-examine his life.

That was why this drive, this pilgrimage to Timmins, was supposed to be just the thing that Charles needed. It would be his way of being alone, without the work, without the booze. Just Charles and his thoughts. Six hours to finally reflect on what his life meant to him other than in the terms of a drunken man's armchair philosophy.

There was only quiet thought and gentle reflection as his car left the sprawling fringes of the city, headed north on Highway 400.

And then, several hours later, the car — the very means of his pilgrimage — broke down.

And Charles was alone.

In the middle of nowhere.

This newest development brought to him the real reason he had never let himself be alone for all those years.

Being alone scared the bejesus out of him.

He was surrounded on all sides, it seemed, by the thick foliage of the Northern Ontario wilderness. Wilderness that grew darker as the sun crept down somewhere behind the distant hills.

Wilderness that threatened to take him back to when he was ten and camping with his parents at Algonquin Provincial Park.

Back to the last time he had really felt *alone*.

Back to the time when he had first learned of *The Bush People*.

"No," he whispered, and it all came back to him in a sudden rush, as if the nineteen years between today and that dreadful evening had never happened at all.

He was returned to that night — back inside the body of a ten year old who was alone and lost in the thick of the night in the middle of nowhere.

He re-experienced it all.

The cold chill of the night wind. The smell of the nearby lake which carried the faint scent of trout. The unending rhythm of the crickets, forever bleating their cries of passion for the night, their chant that there was much more to the darkness than could be seen.

And the knowledge, the dreadful, painful knowledge that his parents were still sleeping in the tent, completely unaware that he was no longer tucked in his sleeping bag, dozing peacefully and protect beside them.

Charles had awoken with a demand from his body that he visit the outhouse. He had slipped out of his sleeping bag and began a quick search for the flashlight. He considered waking his father and asking him where it was, but the urge to go — now — was too great. He unzipped the entrance to the tent and headed down the trail to where he remembered the outhouse to be.

Only, either his memory had failed him or he had missed it in the darkness, because after walking for quite a while, Charles still hadn't found it.

He turned back, the cramps getting worse, and decided that he would wake his father after all.

But he came to a fork in the trail that he hadn't noticed on his way out. He took the one to the right, hoping that it was the correct one. But that trail led to another fork.

That was when he knew that he must be heading in the wrong direction.

He had been tricked.

By *The Bush People*.

The Bush People. His father had conjured them up that very evening in a story told by the campfire. They were the bogeymen of the wilderness that hid behind every tree, beneath every stone. They were numberless, faceless and without mercy. Their sole purpose was to trick little boys by leading them down the wrong paths, deeper into the forest away from the safety of their parents.

He opened his mouth to scream.

But he stopped himself with a sudden thought.

What if *The Bush People* didn't know where he was yet? What if they located their prey by listening for their screams? If he cried out for the help of his parents, *The Bush People* might also hear him and get to him first.

There was no way that he would scream.

The only thing left was to run.

He turned and raced down the path. Branches reached out from the sides of the trail, thin and invisible in the dark gloom. Each time they snagged him, he almost let out a yell, thinking it was a bush person touching him. They whipped at his face as he ran past them and tried to head down the proper trail, the trail that led to the safety of his parents.

The haunting cry of a loon echoed through the forest. To Charles it was the cry of another lost child trying to find his way to safety. Too bad pal, Charles thought. That cry just gave you away. Now they know where you are.

As he was thinking this, he collided with a wall of canvass stretched tightly across the path. He bounced back, sprawling to the forest floor and finally released the scream of terror he had been holding within.

No! he thought. They must have heard me. Now *I'm* caught too.

But then he heard the familiar grunt of his father. A command which was half-snore came from the other side of the canvass wall — which Charles realized was the tent — telling him that it was all right, to get back to sleep. His father must have thought that Charles was still in the tent and had screamed out while having a nightmare.

He quickly ran around to the front of the tent and slipped in. Then he crawled back into his sleeping bag which was still warm from the body heat he had left in it. He nestled there, the bag curled tight about his neck in an effort to keep out the chill of the night air. He lay there unmoving, waiting for the light of day as the pain of his cramps continued to grow.

But he would not go outside again that evening. Not without his parents — not until daytime when *The Bush People* were probably asleep.

And throughout the night, as the loon calls continued, Charles decided that they were *not* calls for help by lost children, but instead cries of pain and horror. The last desperate cries of the poor souls who had already been caught by *The Bush People*.

To keep his mind off of his cramps, he started counting the number of victims they had claimed. He quickly lost count.

Nineteen years later, Charles sat in his car, feeling a sudden urge to urinate. He no longer believed in *The Bush People*, realizing that his father had told him that story out of a fairy tale mentality. The same way that *Little Red Riding Hood* was supposed to teach children not to talk to strangers, Anthony Webster's tale of *The Bush People* was supposed to teach Charles not to wander from his parents when camping.

No, he no longer believed in *The Bush People*. But his fears — of being alone, being lost, and being in the forest at night — remained.

As the need to urinate worsened, becoming a tight unbearable pain, he told himself that he was being sill. Slowly, he opened the car door and stepped out.

The light from the opened car door spilled out onto the highway, pale and yellow. It mixed with the flashing red of his hazard lights. He looked at the light on the frail cracked pavement and then past it to the dark silhouettes of the trees against the grey night sky. He looked up, straight up to see more stars than he could ever see over the city. He saw in them the freedom of open space that this trip had originally promised him.

Freedom that was being threatened by the encroaching shadows of the trees which were far closer to touching the sky than he would ever be.

He hated them for mocking him so.

Unzipping his fly, he urinated in the middle of the highway.

Take that, he thought as his urine pattered on the dry dusty pavement. Piss on you, you stupid barren highway.

As he relieved himself, he kept his eyes on the forest. Black faced, it stared back at him. It was like a two-way mirror. He could sense, with every fiber of his being, that something was there, just on the other side of that blank face, watching him. But no matter how long he stared he couldn't see it. He could only see the trees.

Then, as he finished and zipped up his fly, he caught the glint of steel in the red reflection of the hazard lights. It stuck up from a patch of tall grass across the highway on the far side of the ditch.

Could it be a fallen highway sign?

He took a few steps across the highway and from there could see that indeed it was. Jesus, a highway sign. Maybe it would tell him exactly how far he was from Timmins, or perhaps from the next town. And if it wasn't too far, he could begin his hike.

It was much better than waiting for nobody to drive by all night and reliving ghost stories of his childhood.

His hope renewed, Charles took a few more steps. As he did this he felt a warmth and realized that for the first time in years he was in control of himself, of his fears. As mundane as trekking across a highway to read a fallen sign was, it meant to Charles that he was confronting his situation in an optimistic manner that took his destiny into his own hands. He had had it with merely reacting and avoiding. This time he was initiating a new chain of events.

He stepped off the solid pavement and onto the soft shoulder of the highway. The ditch was shallow, only about two feet lower than the highway, and Charles went through it easily and was on the other side, stepping through the tall grass toward the fallen sign.

Looking down at it, he wondered if instead of telling him anything important it would just be another SOFT SHOULDERS sign. He'd seen enough of them on Highway 144. He took a breath and bent over it.

As he reached down he thought he could feel a boney finger poking at his right shoulder.

Startled, he whipped his head around and saw that it was only a branch from a nearby tree which was sticking out over him. He relaxed again and took hold of the sign once more.

He couldn't read the sign in the dim light and so lifted it, tilting it towards the light emanating from his car.

He felt the boney poking again, this time closer to his neck. Then again. Then something had a hold of his shirt. He whirled around, dropped the sign on his foot, screamed in pain and stumbled forward, twisting his ankle on some unseen stone.

He fell to the ground, hard. The bleating pulses of pain shot up through his ankle to his ears, keeping perfect time with the red flashes of the hazard lights of his car. Another boney finger grabbed at his left shoulder and something pulled on his tie, chocking him.

Quickly, more boney limbs grabbed onto his body and pulled him slowly away from the highway. He struggled, trying to break free, but the chocking tug on his tie made him weak, useless.

In the dim red beat of the hazard lights he detected subtle movements above him which looked like tree branches bobbing to some soundless disco beat — but there was no wind.

He realized that the boney fingers were actually branches from the trees, and that they were passing him along to each other, deeper and deeper into the forest.

As he was being moved, dragged along the forest floor, his head collided with stones and stumps and he wondered vaguely, through the haze of pain and confusion, whether or not he would still be alive when the trees delivered him to *The Bush People*.

Then a new thought occurred to him.

Perhaps there were no Bush People. Perhaps there would be no destination, no end to this mad journey. Perhaps he would continue to be dragged along by the trees, helplessly stuck in yet another cycle until death finally claimed him.

"Please, God! Let the Bush People be real! Let them exist. Please . . ."

ECHOES IN THE NIGHT

More stories

☠

REQUIEM

"SOLD!" the auctioneer bellowed, bringing his gavel down hard, signalling an end to the seemingly endless flow of verbal diarrhea. "To the man in the blue suit for three hundred thousand dollars."

Peter Drebonier III clapped his hands together as his rounded belly hitched with a chuckle he could not contain. *My very own haunted bureau*, he thought. For practically a steal.

Getting the bureau home would not be a problem, but he would have to tip the movers an exorbitant sum so they'd be extra careful with it. After all, Peter had been attempting to get his hands on this little bureau — known in certain circles as "Victoria's Cabinet" — for almost eight years. When he'd heard the museum was auctioning off most of the items in their Victorian wing, he'd been filled with delight.

No, more than delight. Rapture.

The tales told about "Vicky's Cabinet" were legendary. This would push Peter's collection of haunted items over the top, making it, by far, the most envious collection in the world. He knew the security guards working at the museum would breathe a sigh of relief to know that the bureau was being removed from the premises. Peter could barely contain his excitement in getting the bureau home and seeing for himself if the legends were true.

As he watched the burly men heft the heavy cabinet into the back of the moving truck, Peter sighed. Though the cabinet was covered, he could still see in his mind the wide decorative drawers that jutted out from where the thick mirror sat in the fancy wood-carved frame. He couldn't wait to glance into that mirror and see what had frightened more than one security guard from ever entering the Victorian wing of the museum in the middle of the night.

"Let's go boys," Peter grinned, rubbing his palms together. "There's an extra five hundred dollars in it for each of you if we arrive in the next half hour."

☠   ☠   ☠

Peter smiled as he gazed in the mirror at the image of the young woman who was maybe nineteen or twenty years old, with the same blue bow and matching dress that had been described to him over and over by terrified security personnel.

After all those purchases, he thought, after all these years, I *finally* own a real ghost. He looked away from the mirror at his classically furnished living room. Okay, so one of the movers had injured himself trying to get the bureau up the staircase and into the special room where Peter kept all of his allegedly haunted items. And Peter was in such a good mood about owning this bureau that he was willing to let them come back another day to finish moving it upstairs. So he sent them all away, without their tip. "The five hundred dollar tip," he'd told them, "is for when you come back after the weekend and finish the job." They offered to return within a few hours with another man, but Peter thought it would be best if he could have some time alone with his newly prized possession.

Turning his eyes back to the mirror, Peter intently watched the image of the young woman in the mirror, whom the guards had dubbed "Vicky" after the era the bureau had come from. He noticed how she gazed wistfully into the mirror as she fiddled with the bow in her hair. Then, after several minutes, as if still somehow sad, but satisfied for the moment with how she looked, Vicky let go of the bow, shrugged and turned from the mirror. Then her image disappeared.

After another moment, Vicky reappeared in the mirror in the same pose she had first been in, struggling with the tiny blue bow. Peter watched, a chill running down his spine, as she re-enacted the exact same scene he had just witnessed.

How beautiful she looked, this ghost he now owned. But also how sad and forlorn. He felt that he could understand just how she felt as she fixed herself in the mirror. For, many times in his life, Peter too had gazed into his mirror, trying to adjust the way his suit fit the pudgy body he was cursed with, but ultimately realizing there was nothing much he could do about it.

A tear strolled down Peter's cheek as Vicky stopped adjusting the bow, shrugged, turned and disappeared again.

Then the image replayed itself.

Peter watched her all afternoon.

And all afternoon he cried.

It was beautiful.

☠ ☠ ☠

After the movers left for the second time and Peter had tipped them generously, he climbed back up the stairs to the large, over-furnished room where "Vicky's Cabinet" now sat.

Having spent so much time with Vicky over the past few days, Peter had found himself drawn to her in many ways. Like a daughter he'd always wanted to dress up and look pretty — nicer than he'd ever be able to look; like a lover he'd never once had and could only watch and yearn for; like a friend which he had only fleeting memories of as a child. He watched Vicky's image and cried for the fact that his one companion in the world was a ghost from a time long past and could not see him.

Vicky was trapped in her own exact ritual, destined to perform it again and again. Never altering, never seeing what was going on around her. Never realizing how she was being watched, how she was being loved.

Yes, love.

Peter had found himself falling in love with Vicky, in every sense of the word. And why not? They were two similar souls. Each caught in their own rituals of which they could not escape. Why couldn't they be a couple? Sure, he would never be able to act upon his feelings for her, but at least he could dream and watch her.

Watch her, and care for her. Care for her, and long for her. Long for her and lust after her.

Watching her move, Peter had studied over and over the way her small breasts flowed beneath the fabric of her dress. Imagining that she was disrobing rather than fixing her bow, he felt the stirring in his loins and the beginning of an erection.

As Vicky shrugged and turned from the mirror, Peter brought his hand down to rub himself.

The image played itself over again, and Peter unzipped his pants to free his aching erection. Watching Vicky's eyes, wishing that just once her gaze would meet his own, he pumped his erect penis inside his fist and imagined her slipping her dress off of her shoulders.

"I love you, Vicky!" Peter cried aloud, wishing she could hear him. "Oh, how I love you." He closed his eyes as he orgasmed.

When Peter opened his eyes and looked into the mirror, he caught the image of a figure standing by the door. "Oh my God!" he yelled, aware of how his softening penis was exposed, sticky and dripping. It was probably one of the movers having returned. But how did he get back into the house past the alarm system?

Stuffing himself back into his pants, Peter turned, trying to come up with some sort of explanation for what he was doing.

But there was nobody at the door.

"What the hell?"

He turned, looked back in the mirror, and there stood the stranger beside the doorway, glaring. Whipping his head back and forth, Peter confirmed that he could only see the man in the mirror. What the hell was going on?

Dressed in a navy blue button-up front and shiny black tights, the stranger stood at the doorway and stared at Vicky. His blue eyes twinkled and he grinned as he flipped his long flowing black hair from his face.

Just then, Vicky shrugged and turned from the mirror. Only, this time, she didn't disappear. She stopped as if startled by the man. The man's lips moved, as if he were saying something, and he advanced on the girl.

"No. Vicky. Run." Peter heard himself scream. He didn't need to know what the man was saying to understand his intent.

The stranger grabbed Vicky by the shoulder and hauled her to the floor. One hand tearing off his own shirt, the man roughly mashed Vicky's left breast. Seeing her pretty lips quivering, Peter guessed that Vicky was crying or screaming or some combination of the two.

In one solid quick gesture, the man tore open the front of Vicky's pretty dress. Her small breasts hitched as she cried soundlessly. The stranger ran a hand along her cheek, down her neck and over her chest, flicking a finger across a nipple. Then he leaned down and covered one of the creamy white mounds with his mouth.

Viciously, the man bit down, drawing blood.

Falling to his knees, Peter screamed.

☠   ☠   ☠

Something, a bad feeling, woke Peter suddenly.

He sat up in bed.

He listened.

But there was nothing.

Just the same, Peter thought that he should check it out. After all, he didn't want to find that a burglar had broken in and discovered his secret stash of highly valuable haunted artifacts.

As he threw his house coat on and reached into his dresser drawer to pull out the 9mm pistol which he always kept loaded, Peter again regretted not hiring any full-time help around the mansion. He'd gotten rid of the maid, butler and cook as live-in servants after just three days of service. Though they were good people, Peter relished his privacy. He choose, instead, to call them in during the day to clean and cook and tend to his needs. But that decision had also left him alone every night, and potentially vulnerable.

Well, not really. There was the state-of-the-art security system which he'd had installed that kept even the tiniest of intruders from sneaking onto the mansion grounds. It had certainly cost him plenty, but it was worth it for the piece of mind it brought.

What piece of mind? he thought as he excited the bedroom and walked down the hall, the pistol pointing his way. Despite the illegal security system, with its under-the-table assurance that nobody could have possibly made it even close to the mansion alive, Peter was still nervous. While the programs which kept the house under tight surveillance were foolproof they were still part of a newly designed computer system. And computer systems could sometimes malfunction.

Peter couldn't be too careful. He was a wealthy man. And, though he considered himself a decent person, a wealthy man could have plenty of enemies he didn't even know about; people who hated and scorned him not because he had done anything to them, but merely because he was filthy rich and they were not.

When he arrived at the den, he reached in and flicked on the light switch. The room proved to be empty, except for a large wall unit which hosted half a dozen monitors and a large computer terminal.

Walking over to the security system, Peter surveyed it. None of the security cameras inside or out revealed any movement. The system was active to the second highest level, so it was impossible to even get onto the mansion grounds without being seriously hurt, or, more probably, killed.

But, what if someone was inside already?

By pressing his thumb into the fingerprint scanner and simultaneously flicking a switch, Peter engaged the highest level of the system — the one which would not allow anyone to even leave the property. That way, if anyone somehow had gotten past the security system due to a flicker or hiccough in the system's program, they would be stopped on their way out — permanently.

Assured, Peter left the security den and then walked, a little more casually, to the closed door of the special room and listened.

Silence.

Remembering the scene he had witnessed that afternoon, Peter was almost hesitant to peer into the room. He didn't think he could bear to see anything more happen to the girl he had fallen in love with. It was too terrible a thing to watch, helplessly, unable to do anything while she screamed soundlessly for mercy.

Peter paused and took a deep breath, trying to erase the image from his mind.

He opened the door and scanned the room.

Except for the haunted objects — the table and chair set, the phonograph, the old wooden rocking chair, the Gaelic sword hanging on the wall, the empty cedar bookshelf, the Russian army boots, the seascape painting, the charred teddy bear, the purple scarf, the gold-rimmed spectacles, the daybed and the newly acquired bureau — the room was empty.

A flash of activity from the mirror caught Peter's eye.

Remembering the startling vision of the strange man attacking and raping poor Vicky, Peter forced himself to walk over to the bureau. He promised himself that this time he would not run screaming like a banshee if he saw the same horrific scene.

He got close enough to the mirror to peer in.

The reflection revealed that the seemingly empty room was alive with activity. At least a dozen people, of all shapes, sizes ages and cultures were either moving around the room or engaging in some sort of activity with one another.

In the corner by the table and chairs, an old gentleman wearing what looked like a military issue suit sat across from a younger man who looked like an extra out of an early 20's movie. They appeared to be partaking in a conversation which required much effort on their parts.

Beside them, on the rocking chair, sat an elderly woman wrapped in a shawl, staring fixedly at her hands, and rocking to a consistent beat.

Next to the old woman, a young man in a Scottish kilt stood in place playing a soundless set of bagpipes.

A few feet past the Scot, a young blonde woman with gold-rimmed spectacles sat with a knife, waving it a few inches above her wrist, as if trying to work up the courage to press the blade into her flesh.

Standing above the blonde woman was the same dark maned man who had attacked and raped poor Vicky. Sweat gleamed off his bare muscular chest as he leered down at the woman while fastening his belt.

Taking another look at the woman, Peter noticed that her clothes hung on her strangely, as if torn and loose. He realized that this beast of a man must have just finished having his way with her.

Just like he'd had with Vicky.

Vicky.

Suddenly worried because he hadn't seen her, Peter searched the rest of the room. The fascination of seeing so many ghosts had shocked him into momentarily forgetting about the object of his recent love.

Beyond the rapist and his latest victim, Peter spied Vicky sitting in a corner of the room. She was involved in some type of conversation with a young boy who clutched at a teddy bear and didn't seem to be responding to her at all.

Poor Vicky, Peter thought, watching her try to communicate with the boy. Then, unable to watch her any longer, because seeing her torn blue dress brought back memories of the horror he'd witnessed that afternoon, he continued scanning the other ghosts.

All of these people involved in so many different activities.

But no noise.

That, more than anything, was what chilled Peter.

☠   ☠   ☠

Peter awoke a few hours later to a scream.

He clutched the 9mm to his chest and quickly bolted out of bed. Creeping down the hallway, he first checked to make sure the security system was still at its highest level, and then snuck back down to the haunted room.

From behind the closed door, he heard shuffling noises.

"This is it," Peter whispered, checking to make sure the safety was released on his gun. Somebody had somehow bypassed the security system and was after his possessions. Maybe they can get past a glitch in a computer system, Peter thought, but let's see them get past my gun.

Bracing himself against the wall across from the door, Peter prepared to kick the door open, counting in his head.

One, two . . .

A giggle from the other side of the door made him pause.

He listened. There was more shuffling.

Aiming the gun at the closed door, he considered simply shooting through the wood. Perhaps it was too risky to chance getting the door open.

He gripped the pistol tightly and squeezed one eye shut, aiming dead center of the door.

Another giggle.

More shuffling.

Then a deep, hearty voice: "Stop that fucking noise!"

An unintelligible response.

"I said, stop that fucking noise!"

"Eat me!" replied a young feminine voice.

"Would the both of you just be quiet," the voice of an older gentleman.

What the hell was going on in there?

He listened, but there was only more quiet muffled voices and shuffling.

Peter looked back and forth down the hallway, then lowered the gun to his side and stepped forward.

A scream cut through the silence.

A gun went off.

Peter dove for cover up against where the floor met the wall and fired a shot down the hallway when he realized that the gunshot he'd heard was from his own gun. The scream had startled him enough to squeeze the trigger.

Lying on the floor in the empty hallway and bringing the gun up to train it on the doorway, Peter waited a moment. When all he heard was more shuffling and the murmur of voices from behind the door, seemingly unfettered by the gunshots, he got to his feet, carefully turned the door knob and pushed the door open.

As before, the room was empty, except for the objects, and, of course, when he looked in the mirror, the ghosts.

He walked into the room, amazed. A collection of muffled voices could be heard coming from all corners of the room as he moved. Getting closer to the mirror, Peter looked inside and saw the animated figures moving about the room.

But this time, when he saw their feet hit the floor, he could make out the sound of footsteps. This time, when their lips moved, he could hear muffled speech.

He stood and listened. Every once in a while, one of the voices or noises punched through the air with full force.

The scream came loud again, this time with the unmistakable smack of flesh hitting flesh.

Peter spied the room until he found the rapist hunched on the bed over Vicky, his lean muscular arms pinning her own down to the mattress, his naked body heavy upon hers.

Peter screamed as the beast plunged into her.

Vicky's scream met Peters and together their screams mingled and danced in the air to the savage rhythm of the large man's violation.

☠   ☠   ☠

"Get your lazy ass out of my way!"

A foreign tongue responded and there was no mistaking the colourful words which had been chosen no matter that Peter didn't understand the language.

"That's my corner!"

"You had it all day. Up yours."

"Dolly, dolly. My favorite dolly."

"You cheater. Put that piece back. Cheater!"

"With one quick pull of the knife, I'll end the pain forever."

The voices came so loud through the night and down the hall to Peter's room that he couldn't shut them out. Even pressing his hands to his ears the maddening, never-ending torrent of voices rained on him.

No matter where he went in the house, he couldn't escape the sounds of the ghosts. And that, worse than seeing them, was driving him crazy.

Upon fleeing the roomful of ghosts, Peter had run to the security system, hoping to shut it down and run off into the night. But what he found there left him with a cold feeling in the pit of his stomach.

The shot he had fired down the hallway had entered the security mainframe. Whatever else the bullet had done, it had rendered the fingerprint scanner useless so that Peter could not override the system from continuing to run at the highest level.

Making it impossible for Peter to leave his mansion. Since his phone lines were patched through the security system — to ensure privacy from phone tapping, hackers and to monitor all incoming calls — Peter's phone was also inoperable at the highest level without being able to scan his thumb print. And a quick search through the house for his cellular phone was a waste of time when Peter remembered he had left it in the car in the garage which was now off limits.

☠   ☠   ☠

Vicky's scream tore at his heart yet again.

Fixing his top lip tight against his bottom one, Peter lifted the whiskey glass and looked at it before taking the last swallow.

The incessant arguing and screaming and goings on of the ghosts became too much for Peter to handle. The only saving grace of all the intermingled voices was the fact that they helped to blend out Vicky's screams and cries.

But it was taxing.

So taxing that Peter had spent the last twenty hours either drinking or passed out. Remaining in a drunken stupor was the only way he could handle the noise, the constant noise.

But with this, his last drop of whiskey finished, Peter knew that he now had no choice.

He raised the empty bottle like a club and stumbled into the hallway and up the stairs.

Tripping, he fell down, barely feeling the edge of the wooden steps dig into his forehead as he landed. He laid there, listening to the voices. As they sank into his mind he found the strength and conviction to move again.

He got up, clumsily climbed the rest of the stairs and headed toward the haunted room.

Raising his bottle overhead again, he walked into the room and stood looking at the mirror. His voice was raw from hours of shouting and screaming at the ghosts. But all his screaming had done no good. The ghosts, after all, were not aware of him or of the world that Peter existed in. They merely lived in their own world, a world that Peter had become a witness to.

Thanks to that goddamn mirror.

He'd had enough time to figure it all out. It had never occurred to him before, but now, in a drunken haze, it all made sense. For whatever reason, the mirror was like a window into the world beyond the living. That, in itself was quite a discovery. But Peter had unwillingly discovered something else about ghosts.

Ghosts were apparently accustomed to having their own space. What Peter had done by collecting haunted objects was force many different ghosts to share the same haunt. Trapped together for all of eternity, of course they would bicker and fight.

And if the bickering were not enough, there was poor Vicky. What had Peter done to her, thrusting her into the same space as that brutal rapist? Well, maybe he couldn't take back what had been done to her, but at least he could prevent himself from seeing and hearing it twenty-four hours a day.

That goddamn mirror.

With the bottle still raised overhead, he let out a hoarse battle cry and ran at the mirror.

☠   ☠   ☠

Peter awoke to screaming and rolled over.

Strangely, he wasn't in his bed. There was a hard floor beneath him. And something was pressing into his throat. It was painful, and he couldn't breathe, but somehow it didn't stop him from being able to move.

He pressed himself up to his hands and knees and saw that he was beside Vicky's cabinet. Then he remembered where he was when he blacked out.

He'd been advancing on the mirror with the bottle raised when he'd stumbled forward. The last thing he could remember, his head had connected with the surface of the mirror.

Peter looked down at himself, at the huge shard of glass sticking out of his throat. He pulled it out with a sickening slurp and tossed it to the floor. *What the hell?*

"Hey, you, newcomer! Get the hell out of my way!"

Peter looked up at the bare chested dark haired man. The rapist was staring straight at him. He could see Peter. But not only him. All the other ghosts were there, looking at Peter. They could all see him.

"Can you hear me, you stupid ass?" the man said. "Here are the rules: Stay out of my way and I won't beat the crap out of you for fun."

The man moved forward and delivered a roundhouse kick that connected with Peter's head and sent him sprawling across the floor.

Reeling from the blow, Peter realized what had happened. He had accidentally killed himself and become a ghost in this own haunted room.

He stood, dusted himself off and looked down at the piece of glass that had been lodged in his throat. The glass must have been from Vicky's cabinet. Did this mean he was now haunting the bureau with Vicky? Peter then looked up at the man who was advancing on the helpless young woman Peter had come to know as Vicky.

Vicky! For the first time, Peter would now be able to do something to help her. Glancing once again at the shard of glass then again at the dark haired man, Peter smiled.

"Oh, have I got a bone to pick with you."

THAT OLD SILK HAT THEY FOUND

A COOL WIND KISSES ME.

Little by little the sensation rises, becomes more real. The soft light breeze becomes an intense, encompassing cold. But the cold doesn't hurt me — it soothes me. It feels good, comfortable.

Relaxed in the darkness, I realize that my eyes are closed. What am I saying? I realize, for the first time, that I have eyes.

I open my eyes to see the world through some sort of charcoal grey lens. But despite the blurry grey haze I can make out a white landscape and figures moving in the distance. Running and cavorting, their shouts are muffled. I can barely hear them.

I can barely see, I can barely hear.

But I do have life.

It's an incredible feeling — almost overwhelming.

I don't really understand who or what I am, but having life feels good. Knowing that I exist and that I can sense and feel is wonderful.

I try to move, but I can't. I look down.

No!

I don't have legs — just this big round mass.

I look to my sides. My arms are mere sticks. They flail uselessly in the wind.

Who created me? Who gave me this cruel life? Was it those kids who frolic so joyfully in the snow? It must have been. They are the only other ones here. Can't they see what a horrid creature they have conjured? Can't they tell what a torture this life is that they have given me?

"Hey!"

A deep voice calls to me. Who is it that addresses me? Certainly not the children, for they are still ignoring me. The voice sounds much different, much clearer and closer than the voices of the children. My eyes scan the landscape.

"Hey, you! Newcomer!"

Finally, my eyes spot the owner of the voice. He is one like me, off to my left. I can tell he is like me because instead of legs and feet, his bottom is a large white mass of snow. He is built like three large balls stacked upon one another. There is a scarf wrapped around his neck. He has dark lumps for eyes, a carrot nose, two sticks like mine, bobbing in the wind, and several tiny stones in a line which form a horridly ironic grin.

I try to respond, but I cannot make a sound.

"Don't even try to speak. You can't. They didn't give you a mouth," the other one says.

They didn't give me a mouth? Feeble arms, no legs, no mouth. What evil creatures they must be! Why even bother to give me life, then?

"Welcome to the world, Frosty."

Frosty? Is that my name? Did they at least give me a name? I wonder, what is the name of my companion?

"In case you're wondering, my name's Frosty too. For the most part, even if they do name us, we're all called Frosty at one time or another. I guess it's supposed to be a funny name for a snowman. But for the sake of personality, you can call me Oldtimer. I've been alive for ages now. Can you believe that I'm four weeks old? Geez, where does the time go?

"Well, since you're new, I'll give you the low-down. God, it's so good to be able to talk to someone again. Do you know that I've been alone now for almost two weeks?"

Just then, a child runs up to Oldtimer. "Hey now!" Oldtimer says. "Get your paws off of me!" But the child laughs and grabs at the nose.

"YAAAAAAAAARGHHHH!" Oldtimer's scream cuts through my head. I can almost feel his pain as the child wrenches the nose free and runs, laughing, through the snow. Another child, upset, chases after him, determined to get the carrot back.

Oldtimer is quiet for a moment. I wonder if he's okay. I wonder if he's still alive.

I wonder if they create us just to torture us.

"Stupid little brat!" Oldtimer says in a low moan. The anguish is clear in his voice. "I'm okay, now. It hurts, but not so bad as I imagine it was for Sammy."

Sammy? Who is Sammy?

"Sammy was my last companion. He stood not four feet from where you now are. And if you think I'm old, he'd been around from the beginning of time. He was the one who explained to me all about what being a snowman means. Do you want to hear it?

"Well, since you can't speak, then you can't object and you're going to have to hear it.

"If you haven't already guessed, humans created us. We are created merely for their pleasure. From what little I have learned of humans, they do this quite often. They create all kinds of creatures merely to use them as they see fit — and to dispose of in a likewise manner. Sammy told me stories of them breeding creatures merely to eat or to keep as what are called pets. I guess that we're like pets. Except, of course, we can't do much more than stand here. At least their other pets have the freedom to roam around. See this yellow stain at the bottom of my right side? It's a little gift from one of their pets called Spike.

"But what nerve, eh? What gall. To automatically assume ownership of another species — to create another being and then to destroy it for their own pleasure."

Oldtimer is silent again. And it is then that the child who took off after the one with the carrot returns, triumphantly holding the carrot up high. She returns to Oldtimer and sinks the carrot into his face.

He grunts as she does this.

Then the girl turns and looks across at me. She frowns, turning her head to the side. She mutters something and walks forward.

I've never known such fear, such dread. She's coming at me and I can't do anything about it. Trying desperately to cringe and shrink back, I close my eyes and wish I could at least scream.

Her finger sinks into the front of my face. I can feel a painful warmth tearing into me. It becomes a burning sensation — incredibly intense. I feel as if my head is going to explore in a bright burst of white light.

A scream, louder than the one Oldtimer made a few minutes ago, rings in my head. It goes on and on, then Oldtimer yells. "For Pete's sake, cut it out, will you?"

The screaming is coming from me?

I try to stop the noise and sure enough, it stops. I open my eyes to find the little girl smiling up at me. She wasn't hurting me intentionally — she was melting me a mouth.

"Thank you," I say to her, but she is oblivious. She begins dancing around me and singing, but it makes no sense. She sings about a jolly, happy snowman. Her song confuses me. How the hell can a snowman be jolly?

"Hey," I say to Oldtimer.

"So now you have a mouth. I know it must have hurt like a bugger, but it's good you can talk. Sammy said that it was important for us to be able to talk."

"Why is that? I ask.

"Because we have a legacy to pass along. We are created and then can do nothing about our existence. But if we can speak, then at least we can pass along stories to each other. So we have an oral tradition to uphold. We pass along speculative tales of what's to come."

Of what's to come? What is he talking about?

I have to ask: "What happened to Sammy?"

"He was torn apart. Tortured. Smashed to pieces by a gang of kids. It was horrible, watching them do it, listening to his screams. It was, so far, the worst experience I've ever faced — except, of course, for being completely alone these past two weeks."

A muffled yell cuts through Oldtimer's speech. I look to see a group of kids approaching. The girl dancing around me runs in the opposite direction and as the gang nears, I recognize the leader as the one who pulled Oldtimer's nose off.

"Here it comes," Oldtimer says. "Finally, our salvation."

"Our salvation? What are you talking about?"

The first of the kids arrives, kicking a large chunk of snow from Oldtimer. A second kid starts throwing punches. A third kid tears into him, ripping away huge chunks. All along, Oldtimer wails and screams.

It's more terrible than he described.

There is nothing I can do. I look about and see, in the direction the girl ran, a large group of kids coming.

"Hey Oldtimer!" I yell. "Hang in there. It looks like help is on the way."

He moans. "Help? No. No. I'm almost . . . free."

"What the hell are you talking about?"

Punches and kicks send snow flying in all directions. Oldtimer speaks between screams, moans and grunts. "If . . . you think . . . this . . . is a bad way . . . to die," he cuts off for a moment, his voice drowned in an anguished wallow.

"What? What could be worse?"

I can barely see him now through the flailing arms and legs. The little girl and her gang are getting closer, yelling something. Will they arrive in time to save my friend?

"Before he died . . . Sammy told me . . . about, " another wail, "the apocalypse."

"The apocalypse?"

"Yes. The slowest . . . most painful death . . . you can imagine . . . when everything . . . melts. They call it . . . spring. Just pray . . . .that you're not around," there is a long pause as he fights to summon up his last words, "when . . . spring comes."

The second gang of kids arrive and quickly chase the others off with a barrage of snowballs and yells. But it is too late. When they clear the area I can see Oldtimer. He is nothing now but a pile of snow with a few broken sticks, some stones and a scarf.

He has found his salvation.

The kids fuss over the pile of snow and then turn their attention to me, long enough to add Oldtimer's scarf to my neck. They chat for a bit and then leave me to solitude.

Time passes. I can't even cry.

My eyes cast fervently across the fields of snow. My fear is that I'll spot some children off in the distance beginning the ritual of building another snowman. I don't think I could even bear to watch.

I yearn for the mean kids to return. To smash me down the way they destroyed Oldtimer. At least it was quick. I'm remembering when the little girl melted me a mouth and how the burning sensation was the worst I had ever felt. I don't think I can even imagine what it will be like when spring comes and I slowly melt down to nothing.

Now, all I can do is sit here and wait.

And wonder if the torture of melting will be much worse than the agony of knowing now that spring in inevitable.

IDES OF MARCH

A CRUEL, unavoidable empathy has overcome me today.

It had been an otherwise typical day in the middle of March. Spring was coming in like a lamb, and I had the radio deejay repeatedly reminding me of it all morning. Repetitive as his ramblings were, the fact that I was sitting at my desk in the front window and was thus witness to the weather made it all the more redundant.

But I needed the deejay's company; to keep me sane.

I'd been there at the desk near the window all morning on self-appointed sick leave. No, I wasn't ill, but I did have to fill out the tax forms for my wife and I, and if neither of us got on the ball, they'd never get done. On second thought, maybe I was sick. Why else would I volunteer for such a task?

So I sat there, playing with numbers, feeling the warm sun on my face with the easy listening radio station filtering old top 40 tunes to my mind. The temperature outside was just above zero, I could tell, for the previously icy sidewalks were now infested with puddles.

The warm temperature left the remaining snow wet and sticky. The neighbor's eight year old boy, Charlie Fung, was putting the finishing touches on what would probably be his last snowman of the year.

Everything was normal. Everything was fine. And except for the grueling hours and triplicate form headaches that lay ahead of me, it was a pleasant day.

Then this black truck, a Range Rover, I believe, appeared from around the corner of our street and Fifth Avenue and swerved dramatically, taking a long wide turn into the double driveway that we shared with the Fungs.

Two figures sat in the cab, but it was hard to see them through the glare of the sun on the windshield. I was certain that they were drunk, or at least the driver was, the way he'd maneuvered the vehicle. That upset me. I mean, it was barely noon, and already drunk drivers were on the road, endangering lives. I'd never seen this truck before and wondered what connection these yahoos might have with the Fungs, who were very conservative, peaceful and quiet neighbors.

Both figures stumbled out of the truck and confirmed my suspicions about their drunkenness. Their fashion sense wasn't much better. They were large, overweight, and dressed in similar beige full length overcoats, blue baggy ski pants and wool hats with long, floppy brims that kept their faces in shadow.

Together, they lurched toward Charlie, who was looking up at them from his recently created masterpiece. The driver was the first to reach the boy and as he approached, he grabbed Charlie by the shoulder and threw him to the snow.

I sprang from my desk and ran back through the living room, into the kitchen and down the steps to the front door. When I burst into the front yard, Charlie was sitting in the snow, crying silently, and the two men were carrying away the snowman.

When Charlie saw me he started to wail out loud, and I rushed over to see if he was all right.

"The pushed me!" He bawled. "They pushed me! They pushed me!" He continually repeated this phrase, louder and louder. For an obscure moment I wondered if he held any relation to the deejay who'd been keeping me company all morning with his repetitive and redundant words.

Assured that Charlie wasn't hurt, just scared, I looked up to see that the two strangers were putting Charlie's snowman into the back of the truck where five other snowman sat.

I wouldn't be surprised if my jaw hit the snow as I stood there watching.

Stealing snowmen from children? What kind of mentally unbalanced people was I dealing with here? Our world was getting more and more stupid each passing day.

I walked over to the strangers. "Hey buddy," I said, putting my hand on the driver's shoulder from behind. "What's the big ide . . ."

I stopped.

His shoulder was cold and soft, and my hand mashed down into it easily.

He turned to face me, staring at me with big black eyes. *Chunks of coal.* And his flesh was pale white, nothing more than snow. He was sweating profusely. No, not sweating. Melting. His face was melting, and it continued to change its shape before me, the melting water running down his slushy face, the carrot nose beginning to sag.

He said something to me. Or at least he tried to, for his melting face seemed without a mouth. It came out as a mumbled warning of some kind.

Then he pushed me — hard. In the face. His hand was wet and slushy. There was an immediate bitter-cold sensation in my mouth and on my tongue — not unlike a shot of Novocain from the dentist — and I realized I must have eaten a couple of his fingers. The numbing sensation immediately dribbled down the back of my throat.

I stumbled, back, numb, dumbfounded, and fell on my ass.

I sat there in the snow, quiet and wide eyed the way Charlie had been when I first came out of the house, and watched them clamber into the cab again. The truck pulled out of the driveway, backed into a telephone post across the street and then went forward, down to the end of the street, and disappeared around the corner.

I'm not sure where these twisted snowmen came from.

But I certainly know where they're heading.

North.

Although I couldn't at first make out the mumbled word the driver had said to me, I think I've figured it out. It was a desperate, guttural moan, a warning, spoken the same rushed way that way Chicken Little must have bleated, "The sky is falling! The sky is falling!" in the classic Henny Penny tale.

The word I believe the snowman was trying to utter was: Spring.

Spring.

Nothing more than a season to us. But to a snowman, it was the end of the world.

Whoever they were, however they came to exist, Frosty and his friend were heading north and taking as many of their own kind with them as they could gather, the way that birds migrate south for the winter. They were running from the apocalyptic season of spring.

I wondered if they would make it.

Then, shortly after I escorted Charlie to his home and explained the situation to his parents — leaving out the fact that the thieves were snowmen themselves — I came back inside and took my place at the window.

Sitting here in the window again, the sunlight on my face, sweat running down my brow, I begin to wonder something else.

Spring is coming in like a lamb, a soft mild day. But ever since I swallowed the snow flesh of the animate snowman, the numbness has continued to spread throughout my insides. And I've become more and more uncomfortable in the heat. I keep checking the temperature because it feels like one hundred degrees — but it's really only plus three.

I look down at my sweat, at the pools of thick fleshy sweat that has dripped onto my desk, onto the tax forms.

And I wonder if I would be able to find them again.

I wonder if they'd take me with them.

The taxes, Charlie, my wife, none of them seem important to me now.

I'd just like to head north, find a deserted field, and spend the rest of my days standing there, basking in the freezing arctic temperatures.

WIND WHISTLING THROUGH GUTTED PUMPKINS

Halloween stories

☠

BUT ONCE A YEAR

WHEN THE rotting corpse of Ted Winters stumbled into *Gas 'N Stuff*, the little entrance bell tinkled and Harry thought he was either going to faint or laugh.

But he did neither.

Stunned, he watched it lurch toward the front counter with one flesh-gnarled fist raised to the cigarette display.

"Is that really you, Ted?" The word escaped Harry's lips before he realized he was speaking. What a stupid thing to say to a corpse, he thought. But then again, what is the smart thing to say to the corpse of a dear friend?

Ten minutes ago, as he sat there in the deserted convenience store and gas bar located across the highway from the Eastview Cemetery, Harry's worst fear had finally come true. While sipping from his mug of bitter, cooling coffee, Harry couldn't believe what he'd seen through the window.

There was this figure, walking through the fog among the tombstones across the highway. He'd thought, what fool would take a short cut through the cemetery after midnight on Halloween?

Then, as the figure stumbled to the cemetery fence and shakily climbed it, Harry recognized the fool. It was Ted Winters, a friend who had died eight months earlier, and who'd been buried in that very cemetery.

By the time memories of his dead friend, of the funeral services, and of the intense period of grief he'd experienced had filtered back through Harry's mind, the corpse had made its way across the highway and entered *Gas 'N Stuff*.

And now, standing across the counter from him, Ted Winters' unfocused eyes frantically moved all over Harry.

"Ted," Harry said, again surprised he was even able to speak. "You're dead. You can't be standing here."

Slowly, the head of the corpse moved back and forth. The movement brought the stench of its rot to Harry's nostrils.

Leaning forward, Harry threw up all over the counter, the newspaper and his coffee.

Ted, with his fist still pointing at the cigarettes in the glass case above the counter, ignored Harry's latest action. Then again, Harry thought, the act of puking is probably quite uninteresting to a corpse. Once you've seen death, vomit probably seems not worth mention.

The corpse's fist thudded down on the counter as if it were unable to hold the arm up for too long, then it raised it again.

Slowly, Harry reached up, took the brand of cigarettes that his friend used to smoke, and placed them in Ted's hand.

The corpse's eyes rolled around in their sockets, the head pitched back and forth. The mouth worked slowly, and little fetid puffs of air blew into Harry's face.

"What? What?" Harry started to yell, the idea of what was happening trying to force itself to the surface. He's dead, Harry. He's dead, his mind screamed. He can't be standing here. Another part of his mind yelled back: *He's dead, that's true. But he IS standing here. Deal with it.*

Ted dropped the cigarettes on the counter and slouched to one side. At that point Harry knew he had to just go through with this. He could deal with the impossibility of it, sort out the logic, later.

"What is it you want, Ted?"

Ted's crusted lips worked slowly, and as before, only soft puffs of air came out. The corpse lifted his hand to his mouth, his first two fingers forming a "V" as they came to his lips.

Suddenly, Harry understood. Back when Ted was alive, he suffered from some mighty painful arthritis. It was so bad in fact, that sometimes he couldn't even get himself his favourite thing in the world – a cigarette. When that was the case, Harry usually did it for him.

"You want me to get a cigarette out for you?"

Ted's head moved up and down. At one point, Harry thought that his head would actually fall off, the way his chin sunk down into his chest and stayed there a long while.

Harry took the package, peeled the cellophane of, pulled out a cigarette and stuck it into his mouth. Then he grabbed a pack of matches and lit the cigarette.

Ted's eyes got wider and wider as Harry did all this. Finally, he leaned forward and placed the lit cigarette between Ted's lips. Ted's wide eyes closed and the lit end glowed brightly as he inhaled.

When Ted finished the cigarette, his crusted lips formed into a smile. In a low, gravely voice, Ted spoke. "Oh, that's so <u>fucking</u> good. I can't believe I went so long without a smoke. You have no idea, Harry. No idea at all."

Harry almost fell on his ass. Instead, he slowly sank back down onto his stool. Okay, he thought. Okay. My best friend returns from eight months in the grave. He stumbles into my convenience store on Halloween, of all nights. And instead of greeting me, revealing something spectacular about the after-life, or even telling me how much he misses me, he mooches a cigarette off me, smokes it to the stub and tells me how hard it was to go cold turkey for eight months.

What did you want him to do? The second, more logical voice in his head responded. *Did you want him to re-enact a scene out of some "Night of the Zombies" movie? The fact is that he's here, and he's your friend. So what if he needs a smoke – you never held it against him before.*

"Ted. I don't know what to say. How can you be standing there?"

Ted signalled for him to light another cigarette. Harry did so.

"Sorry that I didn't speak, Har, it's just that I couldn't function properly, you know, without a little fix. It . . . took some time, I guess, to get things working properly. I was so stiff from lying there. So stiff. And when I got up, I was so much in need of a smoke. Thanks, Harry. Thanks. I'm feeling much better. A lot less stiff, you know?"

"Ted, why are you here? How can this be?"

Ted puffed on the cigarette, this time more casually. "I don't have much time, Harry. Just let me enjoy a couple of cigarettes before I have to go back."

"Back where? What are you talking about?"

Back to my grave. I shouldn't even be here. If <u>He</u> finds out . . ." Ted's eyes, now slightly more purposeful in movement, glanced out the window toward the highway.

"If <u>who</u> finds out?" Harry reached for his coffee, but then noticed tiny chunks of puke floating around in it. He dumped it out, tossed the soiled newspaper into the trash, and proceeded to clean the counter. Submersing himself in the mundane ritual helped slightly. "Talk to me, Ted. Help me out a bit here."

"I'm dead, Harry. Dead. It means I lie in a box under the earth and I rot. I have nothing now but time. Nothing but eternity to lie there and think – think about all that I can't do, all that I'll never be.

"But once a year, it's my day. Once a year, we're allowed to move, to walk, to talk to each other. Once a year, from midnight until the sun comes up, we can get up and walk around."

"On Halloween?"

"Sort of. Halloween is the evening before what is known as All Hallows Day. During the dark hours of the morning, we're free from death – at least as free as we'll ever be. It's like a romp around the prison yard. Then it's back into the box for another year.

"Do you have any idea how long a year is to a man who can do nothing but lie around and think?"

Harry shook his head.

"I didn't think so. Maybe in time this once a year business will seem more like a treat than punishment. But for now, death sucks, Harry. It really sucks.

"So you'll excuse me, I hope, if I don't sit around and chat politely. After all, time is everything now. And I've wasted enough of it talking." He paused and looked around the store, his head moving with more strength and confidence. "Do you have any beer? I'm dying for a cold one."

Harry moved over to the cooler and took out two beers. "I still don't understand," he said as he returned with the beer and set one on front of his friend and opened his own. "You just lie there rotting? Does that mean you're going to Hello or something?"

Ted shifted forward and leaned on the counter. Again, Harry could smell his dead friend's fetid breath and it almost turned his stomach. "There's no Heaven or Hell. There's only death; and death is death." He paused and looked down at the beer can. "And can you open this for me? My damned arthritis . . ."

Harry opened the can for his friend, who scooped it up and took a deep, long drink.

"Ah, that's the stuff. Anyways, like I said, it doesn't matter what you do in life. When you die, *He* owns your soul."

"He?"

"Death. Death owns all the dead souls." Ted paused to take another long drink. "He's got the monopoly on souls. He's like a collector, a taxman. Each soul is like a dollar bill to him. He keeps attaining more and more. Each individual is just another dollar bill to add to his growing fortune. He doesn't care which soul is which. All he knows is that with each death, he gets another soul. They're all the same to him. And He never loses, He just keeps getting richer and richer – forever."

Ted stopped talking again and fumbled with the cigarette package until Harry lit one for him.

"Thanks. You know, if I could, I wouldn't go back. I'd do anything, trade anything to stay topside with my cigarettes. God, how I miss smoking."

While Ted continued to suck on the cigarette, Harry glanced out toward the highway again. There at the edge of the graveyard, stood a large hooded figure at least nine feet tall. The fog swirled around it as if it were an extension of the robe.

After what seemed like an eternity of staring at this unmoving figure, Harry realized that he was wetting his pants.

"Uh, Ted?" Harry asked, his eyes unable to leave the huge robbed figure. He had no urge to even attempt to control his bladder as he watched the figure. "Ted, who the hell is your friend over there? And why is he watching us like that?"

"Oh, shit," Ted said, stumbling backward. "Oh, fuck, he caught me."

"Who is that? Is that . . . *Him*? Is that Death?"

"No. If you saw Him, you'd be dead already. That's just our Warden, one of His helpers. And he's probably so pissed at me. We're not allowed to leave the cemetery, you know."

"So what are you doing to do?"

Ted didn't respond. Instead, his eyes remained fixed on the figure across the highway. Like before, his lips moved but there was no sound.

As if in defiance of the supernatural spectacle taking place, an eighteen wheel transport down shifted its way into the service bay of the gas station. The rig completely obscured the view of the cemetery.

Harry stood fixed in place, staring at the side of the truck. Then, more willing to accept the mundane, he stepped outside to pump gas.

"Fill 'er up." The driver was already out and rounding the front of the truck. "Do I need a key for the john?"

"No. It's around the side." Harry began to pump gas. The act of doing something normal and routine was helpful, as was the truck driver's matter-of-fact intrusion and gastronomic need. He didn't know what else to do. All he knew was that he was glad the gas tank wasn't on the cemetery side of the truck.

When he filled the tank, the driver was back outside. He paid Harry and quickly moved back into the truck.

Not wanting to be outside when the steel barrier between himself and the graveyard moved on, Harry hurried back inside.

And notice that Ted was gone.

He looked across the highway as the truck started to pull away. The fog swirled around the tombstones and through the fence, but the robed figure was also gone.

Maybe, Harry began to think, *I imagined the whole thing. Maybe I was dreaming while half-asleep or something.*

Then he noticed a lone figure attached to the back of the truck as it pulled out onto the highway. It was Ted, catching a ride.

Staring out after the transport, Harry muttered. "Well, I'll be damned. He's actually getting away."

"Let him go," a deep voice boomed through the store and vibrated in Harry's chest.

He turned and felt his heart skip a beat.

There, in front of the magazine rack, stood the robed figure – all nine feet of him – as silent and still as he'd been in the cemetery.

"Fuck," Harry muttered, and shit his pants.

"I have no time to waste chasing him," the figure's voice rumbled. "Your soul will do."

"B-but you're not Death," Harry said, trying to back away. "And I'm not dead. Y-you can't."

"I can't." As he spoke, fog swirled from beneath the figure's robe, the store was filled with the thick swirling mass, and Harry couldn't see a thing. Seconds later, the fog cleared and they were both standing in the grass. Trees and tombstones replaced the magazine racks, the shelves, the candy displays. "But *He* can."

For the first time the robed figure moved, slowly raising his arm to point behind Harry. At that point, Harry remembered what Ted had told him about Death not caring whose soul was whose – a soul was a soul. And Ted said he'd do anything, trade anything, to be able to stay topside.

A vice-tight grip seized Harry's should and spun him around. He tried to close his eyes, tried to move, to turn the other way.

But it was no use.

As sure as his friend had died, risen from the dead, and then sold him out for the simple pleasure of a cigarette, he knew it was all over.

Harry cried out as he stared into the face of Death.

TREATS

THOUGH THE ringing of the doorbell continued to echo through the house, Percy sat alone in the dark, his arms folded across his chest, and refused to answer the door.

"You're not getting any treats from me," he mumbled, shifting to get more comfortable in the overstuffed chair. When the ringing ceased he heard some grumbles from outside, then the sounds of the kids clambering down the porch steps on their way to beg at other houses for candy and goodies. As they walked away from the house he could see their dark silhouettes moving along the walkway.

Last year, he'd yelled out: "Bugger off!" But that only alerted them to the fact that he was home, and they pelted his windows with eggs and tomatoes.

But not this year – this year he decided to sit in the dark, wait them out and watch. No treats. No tricks.

Why should he give those snot-nosed little brats any treats? What did they ever do for him besides trample his petunias or put the occasional baseball through one of his windows? And if that weren't enough, they were spreading rumours about crazy old Percy who lived alone in that huge house, giving it to the corpse of his dead wife every night.

At that thought, Percy decided it might be a good idea to go check in on Bertha. He got up from the armchair and moved through the dark out of the study and into the hall. The stairs creaked beneath his feet as he climbed, mocking the unheard creaking of his very bones as he moved.

The smell hit him most powerfully, as it always did, at the top of the stairs. Sure, it reached into every corner of his home, permeated every molecule of the air inside his house, but it always seemed worse at the very top of the stairs.

He was already so used to the putrid, rotting odour that it no longer nauseated him – in fact, it had been at least a month now since he'd vomited upon reaching the top of the steps – but his nose still wrinkled and his lips pressed together tightly in an attempt to filter out as much of the stench as possible.

He slowly opened the spare bedroom door, and, even though he knew the smell had to be worse at this point, it never bothered him so much as it did at the top of the stairway. He liked to think it had something to do with leaving the bedroom window open and laying out dozens of containers of potpourri and boxes of baking soda in the room.

The "death" room was lit only by the light which filtered in through the unblinded window. Percy was thankful he couldn't see his poor wife's decomposing body, but the dark brought with it chilled memories of what she looked like. Laying still and quiet in the bed, her thin flesh had seemingly melted itself over the sides of her skull and sunk into her eye sockets, transparent in some spots, like mozzarella cheese heated over a bagel.

Time had not made his task any easier for him. In fact, it had been months since he'd been able to get close enough to kiss her gently on the forehead like he had always done when she was sleeping; and for that he was ashamed. What kind of sorry man couldn't even honour his wife with a gentle show of affection?

All of this, after all, was for her. He'd never gone back on a promise to his wife during their 34 year marriage and he wasn't about to break this one, his last promise to her, no matter how hard it became.

It had been the night before she died when Percy stood watching Bertha toss and turn in her sleep, unsure of whether or not the nightmare she was having could possibly be worse than the reality of the inoperable brain tumour that sat, like a time bomb, in her head. At that moment, Percy could conjure up no worse image than being without his wife, his lover, his best friend, so he decided to let her have her nightmare. It was almost as if the false terror she was experiencing in her dreams was a treat that she was allowed to indulge in. A treat, perhaps, because it was not real, after all, and would be over the moment she woke.

But the reality – the "daymare" Bertha and Percy shared, was something they'd never have the luxury of waking from. Sometimes, in an overwhelming sense of grief, he imagined the tumour sitting in her head like some puffy Jim Henson created monster, gloating at the two of them. "My only purpose," it would half-grunt, half-chortle, "Is to take away the one thing that is precious to you."

When Bertha finally woke, screaming, from her nightmare, Percy rushed to her side, cradled her head in his arms, and told her it was going to be okay.

"No," Bertha cried. "No, it's not going to be okay. Can't you see? Can't you see, Percy? Soon, I'm going to die and then they are going to get me."

"Nobody's going to get you, love."

"Yes, Percy. That's what they do. They wait for you to die and then they crawl in through cracks in the coffin while you lay there helpless. I don't want that to happen. It can't happen!"

Percy rocked his wife back and forth, stroking her head. They had discussed the bugs before. Bertha's greatest fear, which seemed to get worse every day closer to her death, was of having the ground bugs crawl into her coffin and consume her flesh. Their religion forbade the ritual of cremation, so that wasn't an option. All that Percy could do was rock with her in his arms and tell her in a soothing voice that she would be safe from the ground bugs.

This time, though, she wouldn't be pacified by such vague words of hope.

"It can't happen! You can't let it happen!" She screamed, moving away from his gentle hug. Her eyes, almost lit from within by the fear pounding in her heart, bored into his own. "Promise me, Percy! Promise me that you won't bury me until there is no more flesh on my bones."

"Bertha, that's not possible. I can't . . ."

Yes, you can. You have to! Promise me, Percy. Promise me!"

He stared at her, wondering if it were the tumour that were making her act this way.

"Promise me! Please, please, please, Percy."

He looked down at his hands, sweaty and shaking in his lap. "Okay, Bertha. I promise." When he looked back up, her fear was gone, had vanished. With a smile she thanked him and then, amazingly, drifted back into sleep.

As the memory of watching her fall back asleep that night floated through his mind, his eyes started to glass over in tears. He didn't pause to wipe them, he just let himself cry.

"Oh, Bertha," he sobbed. "I won't break my promise. But it's so hard – so hard!"

When the tears were finally over, Percy could hear laughter filtering in from outside. He looked over to the window, remembering again what night it was. The trick or treaters were still out there. He'd better go stand watch again.

Before leaving the bedroom, he decided it would be a good idea to close the window and the blind. There was no telling what the mischief makers could get up to when he wasn't constantly watching.

As he moved down the stairs he was glad that he had shut Bertha's window. It seemed only a matter of time before they tried crawling up the eaves to peek in through the window for a look at her. It was bad enough that he had become the subject for so many childish bleatings overheard in the town. He couldn't bear the idea of "giving it to her" as they said in a laughing rhyme they'd made up about him.

Percy, Percy, quite perverse-ee; gives it to her, shows no mercy.

Some nights he'd lie in bed with that stupid sing-song going through his head and he'd cry himself to sleep.

Percy, Percy, quite perverse-ee, wanted more, so stole a hearse-ee.

Immoral little bastards.

Despite their knack for destruction and painful, dehumanizing rumours all year, one night a year all they needed to do was put on a costume and ring at his door and he was supposed to give them treats? Yeah, right, he thought, settling back down in the armchair. Show them mercy, Percy.

"Screw you," he whispered under his breath. "There's no way you're getting any treats out of me."

Even though he knew it meant spending the evening sitting in the dark in his study and thus losing time he'd rather spend reading from the vast selection of gardening and antique books he and Bertha had collected over the years, his decision was worth it. It was better this way, when he could watch them from the safe darkness of the study. That way, he'd catch them if they tried any of their stupid Halloween tricks.

A new stirring of movement outside the window caught Percy's attention.

He watched a small pack of them loiter up the walkway, thinking to himself: "Doesn't the fact that there are no lights on dispel them?" A smaller, chunky shadow of a kid scurried along a few steps behind the troop. Percy watched as he neared them, then dashed, with a sudden turn, behind a hedge to the left of the walkway.

"What's that little bugger up to?"

He leaned forward in his armchair, squinting, but couldn't make out the short fat kid's figure among the shadows of the hedge.

Meanwhile, as the rest of the pack disappeared in their approach to the house, he listened for the usual childish banter and heavy footfalls on his porch steps, but there was nothing yet.

This was it, he thought. They were getting ready to play a trick – but little did they know he was ready for them.

He got up from the chair and pressed his face up against the window, trying to get a look at the porch, but the hedges and shadows prevented him from seeing anything.

As he was pressed against the glass, he caught a scuttling movement near the ground and quickly turned his head to see what it was.

Just then a shadow dropped in front of the window. Percy flinched back, at first guessing that a rock had been thrown. But when the object hit the window making little more than a quiet thump, he quickly surmised it couldn't even have been an egg.

Confused, he stood and looked at a huge wide strand of a whitish material that ran diagonally across the window. "Toilet paper," he muttered. Of course, it was the oldest trick in the book.

That was it. He made his way through the study and headed to the front door. He'd nab the little buggers in the act.

But a noise coming from the basement stopped him.

They're kids, but they're not stupid, Percy reminded himself. Was this toilet paper and scuttling about the yard just a diversion so that one of them could sneak inside and steal some treats, or perhaps trash the place?

Or maybe they wanted to get a look at Bertha.

How dare they?

Percy ran to the kitchen, pulled open a drawer and dug around for the flashlight. When he found it he moved to the basement door. At the top of the stairs he paused and listened again.

A scraping sound echoed through the darkness.

"You won't be getting any treats from me this year – you hear?" Percy cackled, casting the flashlight beam back and forth across the basement as he descended. "And you certainly won't be getting a look at my dear Bertha."

When he reached the bottom he looked around the pile of storage boxes and then circled behind the furnace. He couldn't detect anything amiss. He did, however, notice that the basement window was cracked open. He shone the flashlight on it. Did the kid really have time to squeeze back out the window before Percy got to the bottom of the stairs? Damn, he thought. I shouldn't have warned him by yelling.

A shuffling noise came from behind him. Percy whirled and faced the crawlspace under the stairs. "I've got you now, you little bugger," he said, advancing on the crawlspace.

Slowly bending over, his back aching in protest, Percy opened the door to the crawlspace and stuck his head and the flashlight inside. Apart from a thick coating of dusty cobwebs, there was nothing immediately inside. But he knew there was a narrow branch leading off under the west side of the house. He pointed the flashlight into the depths of that branch, but the cobwebs were so thick that the flashlight beam was caught on them and could proceed no further into the darkness than a few feet.

Quietly, the shuffling noise repeated itself somewhere in the depths of that darkness.

"All right, you're trapped now," Percy called into the darkness. "You may as well come out."

There was no response.

"For God's sake, kid. I know you're here. Just get the hell out and I'll let you go." But he knew, of course, that he had no intention of letting the kid off that easily. This was breaking and entering, and he'd caught the little bugger red-handed. There was hell to pay for this. Finally, some retribution for all the mischief they'd played on his all these years. He didn't even know where he'd begin.

Contemplating the fear he could instill in the kid, he waited.

Still there was no response.

Percy hunched himself a little tighter and got inside. "Have it your way, kid. Just don't assume that I'll be in a good mood once I reach you."

The cobwebs adhered to his face and he pulled at them, but they were stringy and tough. Despite his disgust, he kept crawling onward, smiling. It would make him very happy to catch the little fatso − he was sure, now, that it was the short fat kid he'd seen ducking away from the others − and show him no mercy whatsoever. He almost laughed aloud as the rhyme came to him. *Percy, Percy, show no mercy; send the fat kid to the nurse-ee.*

Inching along, Percy gave up trying to pull the cobwebs from his arms and face − there were just too many of them, and it was tough enough just moving forward through them. Keeping himself clean of cobwebs down here was as futile as trying to stay dry while treading water.

Every few feet, he noticed a mass of thick white bundles hanging down from the cobwebs. Most were the size of golf balls, but some were as large a tennis balls. Percy steered clear of them. Dead little bugs caught in a spider web were not on his list of things he'd like to touch.

He crawled onward. Where was the little tubbo? How far ahead could he be? He paused and thrust the flashlight ahead of him at arm's length.

His eyelids, thick with cobweb gunk, were harder to open, so he couldn't be sure what he was seeing just ahead. A wide white banner ran across the crawlspace, and as Percy approached it, he wondered at what kind of sick pleasure the kid would get out of toilet papering his crawlspace.

He slugged forward.

When he reached out to break down the toilet paper, his hand stayed stuck in it and the flashlight fell out of his grasp. It bounced end over end and then lay still on the crawlspace floor with the beam pointed back toward him.

He tried to pull his arm free, but it was caught at the wrist. It certainly wasn't toilet paper that held onto him so tight. It was some kind of huge gooey cobweb.

He tried pulling his legs up so he could use his feet to push off the wall and get himself free, but his legs were caught in something too. He turned his head to look at what they were caught on, but a sticky substance held the side of his bald head and he could only turn a little.

As he struggled harder with the webbing, something occurred to him, which he should have caught on to before. If the cobwebs were so thick and unbroken, then a kid couldn't have crawled through them ahead of him. The kid would have broken through all the cobwebs, leaving a clear path for Percy to move through.

Which meant there was no little fat kid inside the house – there never was.

What then, had that thing in the yard been? And what was making that noise in the darkness ahead of him?

He gasped at a strange quiet groan off to his right. It was one of the tennis ball sized sacks. The flashlight beam was pointing directly at it as it shifted and bobbed about, producing a sound he could only decipher as a moan of pain. A chorus of similar quiet groans echoed from the dark corridor he'd just passed through.

His mouth agape, Percy watched the bobbing sack stretch and expand. Then something black and needle-thin punctured the sack from inside. As it emerged, it thickened to a hairy, two inch leg.

Percy turned his head with what little movement he was allowed, unwilling to look at any more of the thing that was undoubtedly hatching out of the sack.

There was more shuffling off in the darkness ahead, and he was very glad that the flashlight was pointed toward him, preventing him from seeing what was making that noise.

The shuffling got louder, closer.

Percy quivered and tried to hug himself with his one free arm. Life is funny, he thought as he passed out. And death – death is the ultimate ironic joker.

After all of Percy's efforts of not giving out any treats on Halloween, the ground bugs – the ones Bertha had been most frightened of – had finally come to collect a treat he'd been keeping from them.

And tonight, they'd collect in spades.

TRICKY TREATER

JUST AFTER dawn on October 31, Danny Kleinner met Satan himself.

Or Satan herself, as it were.

In the guise of a thirteen-year-old child and further dressed in the garb of a nun, Satan appeared as Annie Mason, or Saint Anne, as she called herself. She showed up at the corner store where he worked, demanding candy.

"Hi. I'm Saint Anne. Trick or treat!"

"I'm sorry little girl," Danny said, fingering his goatee. "But we're not giving out candy this year."

The little girl stomped forward and thrust her pillowcase under his nose. "You don't understand. Trick or treat!"

He looked down at her, shaking his head. "Sorry."

Dressed in the cutest little nun habit that Danny had ever seen, the little girl's widened eyes beamed with an excitement that usually only filled a child's eyes on Christmas morning. Little curls of red hair peeked out of the girl's hood, matching nicely with the freckles on her face. Her small, upturned nose and pencil thin lips held an uncertain smile as she peered up at him.

For a moment, Danny realized that she was at least thirteen, and maybe just a little too old to be out trick or treating. But she was too cute to refuse, had there been anything to give out.

The manager specifically stopped giving out treats on Halloween, starting this year. It was too much of an expense to handle, she'd said. So they just had to be strict about it.

Despite the manager's new rule, Danny decided to toss a chocolate bar into Annie's bag. If the loss was noticed the manager would probably write it off as the usual shrinkage which occurred in such a store. The kid was too cute not to give her something.

"Thanks mister." Annie then marched out of the store, and Danny thought that was the last he would see of her.

Half an hour later Annie returned. "Hey mister, how about some more candy?"

Danny stuffed the magazine he'd been reading farther under the counter, his face turning red. How the hell had she entered without sounding the tiny bell above the door? Although he knew that she couldn't see what he was reading, he still felt guilty – as guilty as the first time his mother had caught him reading his father's skin magazines while curled up under the stairs.

Pulling his chair closer to the counter to hide his erection from her, he explained that he'd already given her candy even though he wasn't supposed to.

"But I want more!" Annie shrieked, running down the aisle across from where Danny sat, heading toward the chocolate bars.

"Listen, kid. Why don't you go bother someone else? I already gave you a candy bar."

As he tried to reason with her, Annie began stuffing handfuls of chocolate bars into her bag. With his erection still obviously poking out against his jogging pants, he couldn't bring himself to walk around the counter and stop her.

"Stop it!" he said.

"Come and make me!" she blurted, grabbing more candy. "You can't, can you? Afraid I'm going to see you have a boner?"

Danny's face turned bright red as he sat helpless, watching her fill her bag.

She paused, defiantly looked him in the eyes and laughed. "Must be a really good magazine for your pecker to be stiff this long after putting it away." She advanced toward the counter, his eyes still fixed on his.

Letting out a quiet gasp, Danny leaned away from her. Sure, she looked about thirteen – but her eyes spoke of an ancient and evil wisdom.

Leaning over the counter, her eyes sparkling with mischief, she said. "Don't worry, Mister Boner. I won't tell anyone on you, if you don't tell on me! Deal?"

He nodded.

With that done, she turned from the counter laughing, then ran out the door.

Confused with the quickness of the incident, Danny sat still, very still behind the counter, tallying the time it took for his erection to subside.

"Damnit," he cursed, looking at the half-empty shelves of chocolate bars. There was no way of getting away with this. How could he explain that a thirteen-year-old had robbed the store while he sat behind the counter doing nothing to stop her?

He got up from the chair and walked over to the candy bar rack, beginning to shift the inventory around, trying to make it look as if it weren't half empty.

"Hi, Mister Boner!"

The voice came from behind him. He whirled around.

"I see that your pecker is down for the count? What's the matter? Not interested in your girlie magazine anymore?"

"What?"

"Maybe you're interested in me."

He backed away from her, his back against the candy bar rack.

"Get . . . out of here. Now, before I call the cops!"

"You're *not* going to call the cops. And we both know that, don't we?" She leaned forward, and for a second her eyes took on a lusty adult appeal, and Danny felt a stirring in his groin.

God, no! Danny thought. *This is a child. She can't possibly be having this effect on me. I'm scared, not horny, for Christ's sake.*

"No. It wouldn't look good if the cops showed up and you were standing there with your pecker pointing like an arrow straight at a sweet innocent child like myself."

"Damnit!" Danny knew that she was right, and fought at the rising erection as she continued to hold his gaze, mesmerized by her sudden lusty charm.

105

Annie then danced around the side of the counter, laughing. She grabbed the magazine he'd been reading earlier. "Oh," she blurted. "*Busty Blondes!*" This is a good one." She stuffed it into her bag. She then slid his chair over and stood on it so that she could reach the high shelf that held the rest of the adult magazines. Reading off the titles in a mocking voice, she stuffed them all in her bag.

Again, he was helpless. Instead of moving closer to stop her, he began to inch his way toward the back of the store

So far, she hadn't noticed.

"Oh . . . cigarettes." Annie chortled, beginning to pull packets of cigarettes from the shelf behind the counter and tossing them into her bag. "This is great."

Danny reached the back of the first aisle when Annie finished with the cigarettes and again turned her gaze on him. She leapt down from the chair and was at his side almost immediately.

"Where do you think you're going, Mister Boner?"

"Uh, nowhere." He froze in place as her hand reached out to him. *Please don't touch me!* he thought, over and over. *Please don't touch me!* He closed his eyes.

"Good, 'cause I'm not quite done here." Her voice began to trail away, but he kept his eyes closed. "Oh, goody. Condoms. Aspirin." Her laughter then sailed past him as she discovered something else. "Wine! Beer! All right!"

He opened his eyes to find her standing before the refrigerator, filling her bag with six-packs and magnums of wine.

Being that far away from him, and with her back to him, he felt it was time to make his break for it. It was now or never.

He hurled toward the front of the store, and almost made it to the door when something grabbed at his jogging pants and tore them completely off, tripping him in the process.

Stumbling forward, he fell while trying to cover himself, and whacked his head on the chip stand on the way down.

Annie laughed, standing beside him holding his jogging pants in one hand like a trophy.

"Goodnight, Mister Boner," she said as he blacked out.

☠   ☠   ☠

"I'm horny," the words filtered into Danny's mind through the darkness, but they weren't enough to bring him around.

Something soft and warm touched his stomach and then slowly moved down. He began to wake up then, feeling not only the careful dance of fingers along his hardening penis, but the cool of the floor against his naked back. Danny also felt the trickle of blood running down his forehead where he'd struck the chip stand. He moaned.

"Mister Boner, you're awake. Good."

He recognized the voice immediately. He didn't have to open his eyes to know that it was little Annie. Nor did he have to speculate to know that little Annie Mason wasn't a young girl at all. She was ancient and reeked of power – she was eternal – she was the night. She was lust, greed, hunger, envy – she was everything that Danny desired, everything that he hated. Everything that he wanted.

And she wanted him.

He cracked his eyes open to find her crouched over him. Her fingers moved up his chest and touched his face.

"You were asleep for a long time. But now that you're awake, I have one more trick to perform."

"What's that?" he asked, feeling his soul being caressed by those eyes.

"Kiss me," she whispered and moved back a little.

He leaned forward.

The hunger to have her grew. The longing, the intense passion was overbearing, even though he knew it was wrong. He'd been alone for so long. Alone and scared. Her eyes sparkled as she gazed at him, and he knew that he could find everything he'd ever longed for in her touch.

She moved away again. "Kiss me, Danny. But first there's something I want from you."

He sat up, but was still too far away. He kneeled, moving toward her. He had to have it all, now. He had to merge with this power held before him.

"Anything,"

She stood, backing away. "Give me the gun."

The gun, he thought. The handgun that he brought into work to protect himself during the overnight shifts: His one safety precaution in a city wracked with violence.

"Why do you want the gun?"

She pursed her lips. "Just give me the gun and I'll give you . . . everything."

Danny stood, his erection throbbing, and moved toward her.

"First, give me the gun."

He stepped backward, behind the counter. "You could have taken it while I was unconscious."

"I could have, but I want you to give it to me."

She said it in a way that carried a double meaning. He gulped and reached under the counter and picked it up.

"Promise me," he said.

"Promise you what?"

"That if I give you the gun, you'll . . . you know."

"I promise," she purred, reaching forward. "Give me the gun, and I'll fuck you, Danny. I'll fuck you like you've never been fucked before."

He reached out, handing her the weapon.

"That's it, Danny." She took the weapon and laughed. "That's it, Danny. Now, wait here and I'll be right back."

She dashed out the door, leaving him standing there mesmerized – longing for her – filled with the memory of her touch.

He wasn't aware that she had left and returned, only that she was in front of him and that he could barely contain his eagerness.

"I'm back, Danny. Now you can kiss me."

His heart pounded heavily in his chest. He could not believe the power he felt, the intense longing she had created in his soul. After a life of emptiness, it was all before him, offered to him in one simple gesture.

"Kiss me, Danny." She backed away slowly.

He moved forward, closing his eyes.

"Kiss me," he felt the breath of those words on his lips and his erection ached with longing for her.

Finally, his lips touched hers.

As quickly as the kiss began, she backed away.

The tinkling of the tiny bell above the door sounded.

Danny spun around in time to see two police officers storming down the aisle, batons raised.

He didn't feel them strike.

☠   ☠   ☠

Danny awoke to the sound of a car door slamming, this time feeling the cool kiss of vinyl on his bare buttocks and the cold hardness of steel around his wrists, which were locked behind his back. His vision was blurry, but he could make out the metal grid separating the back seat from the front.

The officers got into the front seat of the car.

"It takes all kinds," the man in the driver's seat said, shaking his head.

The passenger sucked in his breath and blew out a long, loud gust of air. "Thought that maybe we could get through one Halloween without some perverted freak ruining it."

"How can we keep the streets safe with assholes like him out there? What kind of fuck-up gets off on distributing booze, porn magazines, pills and cigarettes to kids who can barely tie their shoes?"

The cop in the passenger seat turned and glared at Danny. "You get tired of the standard razor blade in apples?"

Danny shook his head, beginning to cry.

"What possesses you people to hand out those things to minors? What were you thinking when you put a loaded handgun into a little boy's Halloween bag?"

Danny gasped, his tears further blurring his vision. It was clear now what little Annie was doing when she left the store.

"He shot two of his friends, you lousy bastard. One's dead, the other is in intensive care. And do you know how many cases of alcohol poisoning were reported from children in this neighbourhood?

"And if that wasn't enough, you go exposing yourself to that little girl. It's a good thing we got there in time, because had you even touched her . . ."

"Frank," the other cop interrupted.

"If I wasn't in uniform, I'd probably have killed you for all that you did."

"Frank, careful what you say."

"To hell with protocol. I mean it. I have half a mind to ditch my badge right here – right now – and take off those cuffs and beat the life right out of this prick.

"We have a responsibility to our kids, pal. We have to protect them from the cold, harsh adult world – not flaunt the evils of it in front of them, not hand it out to them."

Danny turned his head, he couldn't bear to look at the infuriated officer any longer, couldn't stand to listen to what had happened that evening.

But what he saw out the window was worse.

Annie Mason was standing on the street corner, a cigarette in her mouth, a whiskey bottle in one hand, leaning against a lamppost. She winked and pursed her lips at him.

"Happy Halloween, Danny," her lips mouthed. Even though he shouldn't have been able to hear her, this far away in the sealed police cruiser, her words were powerful and loud in his ears. "I promised I'd fuck you."

As the police car passed her, Danny caught a fleeting glimpse of her transforming into the hideous being she really was. Her laughter followed, etching itself to Danny's brain, refusing to be forgotten.

TWO HANDS CLAPPING

Stories written with others

☠

TIL DEATH DO US PART?

(With John Strickland)

DAVID RETURNED to the keyboard to update the reports he had so recently been compiling on the afterlife. But he couldn't calm himself long enough to type the words in.

He just couldn't believe what had happened.

He rose from the computer monitor and walked away from it, from the only source of light in the room. In the dark he easily found what he was looking for: the tall thin bottle of amber delight that helped him get through times like these.

Placing his lips on the scotch bottle he contemplated the blinking cursor on the computer screen. A flashing beacon, it called him. He quickly downed the last inch left in the bottle and found himself at the keyboard, a little less shaky, a little less excited.

Was it just my imagination? David wrote, the green letters on the screen blinking back at him. Oh Mom, was it just my imagination, or did I really see you standing there? David stared at the screen a long time, the stark words sobering him up more effectively than any pot of coffee ever could.

And as he sat there, the image of what had just happened playing itself over in his mind.

He'd just booted his computer on, reached over to replace the boot disk with the data file disk, when he felt a distinct presence in the room. There was no mistaking the way that the air seemed to shift as if something had suddenly formed, taking up a spot in the room where before there had been nothing but empty space.

And then there was the feeling of being watched. As if whoever, whatever was watching him affected him physically — as if the act of being looked at could actually touch him somehow. His skin rippled with gooseflesh and he sat there unmoving, afraid to even blink.

After years of combining countless seance rituals with scientific measurements and equipment, had he finally contacted a spirit of the dead? Was that what was watching him? Was that what was standing in the darkness behind him? Twenty years of research and it all came down to turning and seeing for himself. But he couldn't bring himself to do it — not yet.

His mind had lingered on the feeling of eyes penetrating the back of his neck, the weight that seemed to share the floor with him, the mass that shared the air of the room. He concentrated on these feelings, tucking them all away into memory and took a breath.

Then he'd turned — the feeling of being watched growing intensely — and there she stood, his mother. Although dead for over six years, there she was, arms outstretched to him. A gentle, loving smile on her face and her eyes wrinkling as she smiled at him, her lips mouthed silent words. *Davy*, she seemed to say. *Davy*. Then she'd faded, becoming transparent, and completely disappeared.

After what seemed to him a very long time of rehearsing the scene over and over in his mind to be sure he missed no detail, his stiff fingers returned to the keyboard. He typed, but his hands seemed to have become dislocated from his brain. After all this time, why have you come back, and why now?

"You know why . . ." The voice, so small that David wasn't certain he had heard it, flowed from some dark corner behind him. Slowly, deliberately, David turned around in his chair. His eyes probed the dark corners of the basement where he had set up his home office and lab and flicked on the desk lamp. The light spilled across most of the one room basement, but he found nothing, nothing at all, absolutely nothing.

He thought. For though he saw nothing in the room, he could again feel the presence. The air shifted again, and although he couldn't see her this time he knew, just from the feeling, that she was back. He pictured her standing there, looking at him, her lips mouthing his name over and over.

He turned back to the keyboard, back to the report he had been compiling. His fingers once again did their slow dance on the keys. Is it because of Dad? he typed.

If he expected an immediate reply, he was disappointed. His breathing stilled and he let his mind relax for the quiet, sibilant tone of his mother's voice. The voice did not come, but he knew she was still there — he could still feel her presence. Patiently, he waited. After twenty years of research and experiments, a few seconds of waiting meant nothing.

The sharp, staccato strokes of his dot matrix printer made him jump. He nearly cried out, but stopped himself.

DAVY, YOU KNOW IT IS, was printed in capital letters across the top of the page.

He spun in the chair and eyed the empty scotch bottle. In the dim light of the basement for an obscure second it almost looked as if it were full again, and David nearly flung himself at it. But a second later, he realized that it was his imagination.

Oh, but what if everything else had been his imagination as well? Perhaps once, he thought. But not anymore. Now he had undeniable proof. Seeing things, and hearing voices could be dismissed as the work of a tired mind. But finally there was some physical evidence — the printout.

But more than that, he was now positive of the reason she was back. Because of Dad. Which meant Dad would be back too. And soon David would be caught between them. Just like before. He sighed, then faced the computer screen and began typing.

What do you want me to do, Mom?

He sat back and waited. He licked his bottom lip as his eyes trained on the computer screen, then on the printer, then back again. The image of her reaching out to him filled his mind, and he thought he could feel movement in the air behind him. He cringed at the thought of her reaching out to touch him, then closed his eyes and told himself to relax — this was something he'd wanted for years.

The first thing he saw, when his eyes opened, was that the computer screen had filled completely with three words. Over and over they repeated without any spaces between him, and the screen scrolled madly to keep up with the repetition of the phrase.

MAKEHIMSTOPMAKEHIMSTOPMAKEHIMSTOP

"What is it this time?" David began to say, but only got out the first two words before a noise behind him stopped him short.

Beyond the reach of the desk lamp, the stairs to the basement groaned softly, and a musky smell filtered into David's nose. He knew, with certainty, that he and his mother's presence were no longer alone. A second presence had joined them and the faint scent of Old Spice aftershave gave away the second presence's identity.

The phone rang, sending vibrations through David's spine.

"Dad?" David whispered, thumbing the computer monitor off. He stared for a second at his reflection in the dull monitor. He stood up slowly and walked over to the phone as it rang again.

He let it ring once more, licked his top lip, then picked up the receiver.

"Dad?"

"David," The voice was familiar, although faded and distant as if it were a call made from a foreign country across a sea of hundreds of raging storms. For an obscure second an imagined Bell Canada advertisement ran through his head: *Reach out beyond the grave and touch someone.* David looked across the room at the paranormal recording equipment he'd had sitting on standby all this time. It was showing readings of the expected drop in temperature, unstable shifts of humidity as well as the sliding atmospheric pressures associated with spirits of the dead. He really should start recording everything.

"Yes, Dad?"

"Tell your mother that if she has something to say to me then she can say it to me herself."

David shuddered and dropped the receiver, his mind racing back to the first time his father had uttered those very same words to him.

It had been over thirty years ago.

Eight years old, David was far from the experienced paranormal researcher he would one day become, but as he poured his milk onto his cereal, noting the timing and frequency of the snap, crackle and pop noises it made, he was every bit the analytical scientist.

George Stevenson sat at the breakfast table across from his only son, proudly watching David's morning experiment. He looked as if he were about to say something encouraging and fatherlike when Dora Stevenson walked in. His proud smile quickly cooled to a grimace and he tilted his head down to regard the morning paper.

"Good morning, son." David's mother said, leaning down to kiss his cheek. She then walked past her husband to the coffee machine and poured herself a cup.

David looked at his parents, knowing immediately that there was something wrong, something lacking from that morning's family ritual. And even though he didn't understand it, he knew they had been fighting. Again.

When Dora opened the refrigerator door, a huge frown came upon her face, wrinkling her forehead. She pulled out the empty cream can and put it down hard on the counter top.

"David," Dora said. "Would you tell your lazy father that the refrigerator is not a place to store empty containers."

"David," George said. "Please tell your mother that if she has something to say to me, she can say it to me herself."

David poured more milk onto his cereal, wishing that he could make the snap, crackle and pop loud enough to drown out the ensuing argument.

As the years passed, David became certain that the fighting would not end until they both killed each other in a ridiculous fight over who lost the television remote control. Perhaps that was why David never left home. He felt a need to stay close and protect them from each other. Whether it was out of some self-imposed guilt or a sense of strict responsibility, he didn't quite know. All he knew was that he felt a need to place himself between his parents — it was the only place he'd ever seemed to really fit in.

He went to a local college and got his degree there. And when he found work, he made sure it was close to home so he could stay nearby and continue to become trapped in the middle of their bickering. A relationship was simply out of the question. Not if a relationship was nothing more than going through a daily drill of arguments about toilet seat lids, misplaced sections of the newspaper and slightly burnt toast.

Every choice he made was for them, and not him. All his life they did it to him — made him give up what he truly wanted, truly needed in life — without ever once realizing it.

But for all he did, for all he loved them and all they each loved him they both died needlessly. On what was supposed to be a Sunday drive in mid-January, his parents' car spun out of control to plummet off of a ravine and into the cold deep waters more than 60 feet below.

Quite often, David fantasized about the argument they must have been having as the car crashed through the guard rail and sailed through the air. They were probably so pissed off then — not so much that they were going to die, but that there was so little time to get all their little jabs in before crashing the surface of the icy river.

He imagined his mother going into her routine of "I told you so's" as the car spun out of control while his father simply let go of the wheel, giving up on the hope of surviving, pressed his hands to his ears and called out in a loud sing-song voice like he had so many times before: "I can't hear you!"

Time and again, the image of them bickering in the brilliant fashion they had developed over the years played itself in his mind. Right until that very second of death, they must have played out their ritual — and at times he thought of them endlessly falling, trapped in that car, and fighting. An eternal, enclosed argument with no winner. Not even death, who wouldn't have them ruining the peace of the afterlife.

"<u>David!</u>" his father's voice barked through the receiver. "<u>David! Where are you? Pick up the phone!</u>"

David returned the receiver to his ear. "I'm here, Dad," he said with a calmness he did not feel.

"<u>Is your mother still there?</u>"

"I don't know. I haven't heard from her for a few moments." It was amazing, David thought, that despite the shock and impossibility of his dead parents communicating with him, he'd easily fallen into the old role of being the go-between in their arguments.

Almost as if challenged, the staccato bark of David's printer started up. DAVID, MY SON, I AM NEVER FAR AWAY FROM YOU AND WILL ALWAYS LOVE YOU, it read. TELL YOUR FATHER THAT MY LOVE FOR YOU WILL NEVER DIE, EVEN IF HIS DOES.

The voice from the telephone was equally terse. "<u>Tell your mother that her posturing doesn't impress me in the least. I may not say it as often as she does, but I love you just as much as she does. I promise to always love you, and as I think you know, I keep my promises.</u>"

David shook his head in frustration. "Mom, Dad, I think you both know that I am trying to get some work done here, and I would appreciate a little co-operation." Somewhere, at the back of his mind, David wondered just how many times he had spoken those same words when they were both still alive.

YOU NEEDN'T WORRY ABOUT ME, DAVID. I'M THE MOST CO-OPERATIVE PERSON IN THE WORLD. WHY JUST LOOK AT ALL THOSE CHURCH COMMITTEES I WORKED ON! I AM THE VERY HEART OF CO-OPERATION.

"You'd think to listen to her that your mother invented co-operation. Let me tell you, son, that I know what co-operation is! You don't get to be manager of a bank without learning about co-operation. Go ahead and ask me anything, anything you like."

"The only thing I want to ask you at the moment, Dad, is to be quiet and listen to me." David hissed the words into the telephone receiver. "I've been putting up with this bickering all my life. Why can't the two of you just stop it, just stop this bickering for a little while and help me prove my theories about life after death?

"I'm onto something here, guys. After spending my whole life researching the existence of life after death, you're here communicating with me. Finally, I have made the connection I have needed. Finally, I have a link into the afterlife. Finally, I can become someone — I can make a difference. I can change history forever. Can't you see that?

"So can you please stop bickering long enough to help me? Long enough to answer a few of my questions?"

WELL, I'M CERTAINLY READY TO STOP BICKERING, EVEN IF YOUR FATHER ISN'T. The words streamed out of the printer. I WILL DO ANYTHING FOR YOU SON, ANYTHING AT ALL.

"Don't be fooled by that phoney devotion, son," the voice, distant but strong, said through the telephone. "Your mother is an expert at making promises she has no intention of keeping. I should know, after all, she made most of them to me."

IF YOU WANT TO TALK ABOUT FALSE PROMISES, LET'S TALK ABOUT ALL THOSE TIMES YOU SAID THAT WE'D . . .

"Guys, please!" David yelled. "Please!"

Simultaneously, the voice and the printer responded.

YES, SON?

"<u>Yes, son?</u>"

"I've been trying to contact you for three years. What made you decide to come back, to finally answer me? How did I succeed in reaching you?"

WELL THAT'S SIMPLE, SON. SO SIMPLE THAT EVEN YOUR FATHER COULD ANSWER THAT ONE.

"<u>Shut-up, Dora. I don't need this crap from you.</u>"

"That can't be all it takes," David said. "Because if so, why didn't you come sooner? I've been trying to contact you for years. Why now?" So many other questions ran themselves through his head. *Could you hear me trying to contact you before? Or were you unaware before I reached into your world? How are you using the phone and the computer to communicate? How can you affect the physical world? What exactly is the spiritual world? Or is it spiritual at all? Do you take on a solid form? Are your presences here merely spiritual, while you exist in a different form in the afterlife?* He had to try not to think too far ahead, or he wouldn't pay attention to the answers they were giving him now.

"<u>It's not as simple as your idiot mother says, David. It was the way in which you contacted us that reached us. But it was not only that, it was the time, the place, the mood. And we can just as easily be commanded back, son. It's quite sophisticated despite the straight forward nature of it — it just has to be timed precisely, and you have to keep several things in mind. Get a pen or something, son, because there will be many things for you to record.</u>"

THERE GOES THE PROFESSOR MAKING THINGS MORE COMPLICATED THAN THEY HAVE TO BE WITH ONE OF HIS LECTURES. DON'T LISTEN TO HIM, DAVY, IT'S REALLY NOT THAT DIFFICULT. LET ME TELL YOU HOW IT IS DONE WITHOUT ALL THAT BIG TALK.

David sat up. "Mom. Dad. Please!"

"<u>I am not making things complicated, Dora! I'm stating the truth, which is more than I can say for you. We're dead now, so you can't continue to try and shelter him from reality and truth. You can't go on trying to give him nothing but simple answers to difficult questions, it just won't do.</u>"

"Guys, please . . ."

WELL YOU JUST CONFUSE HIM WITH YOUR BIG WORDS AND BIG TALK. YOU NEVER SPOKE TO HIM WITH LOVE AND TENDERNESS. THE ONLY WORDS YOU EVER OFFERED HIM WERE OF THE HARSH AND COLD WAYS OF THE BUSINESS WORLD. WELL THERE'S MORE TO LIFE THAN THAT YOU CLOSED-MINDED JERK.

"Please, guys. Mom? Dad?" David leaned forward, gesturing, hoping to somehow catch their attention. "Can I say something?"

"Closed-minded? Why I'm the most open-minded man there ever was. Wasn't I, son?"

GO AHEAD, DAVY, AND TELL HIM THE TRUTH. HE'S CLOSED-MINDED ISN'T HE? WELL, DAVY, ISN'T HE?

"Answer us, son."

DAVY?

David drew in a deep breath and stood, yelling at the top of his voice. "I had enough of this bullshit while you were alive. My entire life I put up with the two of you. I gave up everything because of you, and I'm not going to put up with it anymore — especially not when you're dead. You're dead, for Christ sakes! You're dead! Shouldn't the bickering be over? Can't you just shut up? You're dead. I shouldn't have to listen to one more word out of either of you. You're dead, dammit! Dead! So shut up! Shut the fuck up! Please! Would you both just shut up!"

There was a long moment in which David waited for some sort of reaction, his chest heaving from the long-winded yelling. He'd been holding a speech similar to that his entire life. He never thought he'd use it on them years after they'd died.

"I don't have to be told twice to shut up," his father said over the phone.

NEITHER DO I, his mother wrote over the printer.

Then there was silence.

It was a long, long time before David realized the silence would be eternal.

It was not very long after that, he realized he had found conclusive proof of life after death, only to have it taken away from him at his own insistence before he'd had any real answers.

He sat looking at the paranormal activity instruments, all of them showing that nothing extraordinary inhabited the room with him. Because their argument distracted him, he'd never even recorded the data they'd been showing. He stared at the machines and shook his head.

His parents had done it to him, *again.*

MARK LESLIE

IT CREEPS UP ON YOU

(With Carol Weekes)

HE SLOWED the car along Parson's Road to view his old house from across the street. The last occupants had left the place back in 1976, and from what he'd heard, in a hurry, too. Some said it had been due to bankruptcy, another said divorce, but John Ingram knew better. Something had driven the last family out, and he thought he could understand what. When he'd lived in this house at 24 Parson's Road as a child, everything had been normal—until one fateful night many years ago.

It had everything to do with the comic book he held in his hand. He tapped it against one leg, hating it, afraid of it, but also relieved to have found it. It wasn't the same book his brother Martin had bought back in 1975, but it was a continuation of the toxin, an unusual and frightening kind of poison that had begun to ruin his life two decades earlier.

He crossed the road towards the house. Dead leaves crunched under his feet. He watched the windows for any sign of movement. His lips pressed into a tight line and he regarded the house, swearing he was finally going to see this through to the end.

☠ ☠ ☠

It began again when he stopped into a pawn shop to purchase a small mantel clock for his apartment. The shop was built back at the turn of the century with small, paned windows peering into a dim interior. He'd picked up the clock and was on his way back to the cash register when he spotted the comic.

His heart gave a jolt. Adrenaline, as sour as old garlic, slammed into his stomach. He gripped the clock to his chest, feeling his fingertips tingle.

Authentic Horror Comics.

It sat atop a column of newer comics, its faded color seeped into the cover, letters carved in streaked, bloody red.

"It's an oldie," the proprietor said. "Not as old as some of the *EC*'s I've had, or *Marvel*, and *Dell*. I've even had originals with young Bradbury's tales, but they went fast."

"Huh?" John snapped back into reality. "Where did you get this?" Needles of white light played across his vision.

"Woman brought it in, three, maybe four months ago. I had it in the back with a pile of old books."

"When did you put it out?"

The old man regarded him. "This morning. Why? I take it you don't like the old horror comics? Everything today is robo-this or tech-that. What happened to things like good old ghosts?"

They go into hiding until the right person comes along, John thought, feeling a little sick. He shuddered and pulled out his wallet. "How much do you want for it, and the clock?"

The proprietor grinned. "Can't resist in the end, eh? There's nothing like being a kid curling up in bed with one of these things and a flashlight. Give me a dollar-fifty for the comic. The clock will be fifteen, plus tax. That comic...I haven't seen no others like it. Not by this publisher."

"I have," John whispered. "Back in '75."

"No kidding?" The proprietor wrapped the clock and secured the package with hemp cord. He handed it, and the comic, to John. For a second John thought he felt the comic tremble beneath his fingers, a whisper of pulse moving through yellowed pages reeking of dead, faded ink, moths, time. The date in the top right corner read: *October 96: featuring Phantastical Fiction and Grueling Art by up and coming names in the business.* He allowed his eyes to trace the cover and noted a man digging into a moon-washed grave, his face slashed in black and green shadow, his eyes livid and his mouth stretched into a leer. Below the illustration sat the words *Continuing with the tale IT CREEPS UP ON YOU: Part B*.

"This can't be happening, not after all this time," he uttered. He hurried from the store towards his car. Wind tickled at his hair and pried at his clothing. He had the undeniable feeling that, should he bring this comic back to 24 Parson's Road, events would begin to happen again. He had to find out. And if nothing occurred, he'd chide himself for still being so fearful, superstitious, and yes...hopeful. If nothing happened he'd dump the comic in the nearest trash bin, go home, and forget about *Authentic Horror Comics* and the disappearance of his older brother Martin, before he went crazy dwelling on it any longer.

He drove with hardened eyes, ignoring the curled comic rolling back and forth on the passenger seat...fluttering beside him, although the windows of the car were all closed. He followed the river until he reached the house.

"Do it and get it over with," he sighed, and grasped the comic book, his breath coming in cold, white bursts.

☠   ☠   ☠

He stood in the yard, and swore he could smell all of it again: the musky odor of age and weather beating at the structure, (he'd tried to come back here two years ago and had run...run from something he hadn't seen, but which had hung like a pall over the place); the stink of aged fear and buried secrets. Crab grass tickled at his shoes. Spiders had burrowed everywhere, giving the eaves and shingles a gauzy appearance. He stopped in the front yard and forced himself to open this latest edition to where *IT CREEPS UP ON YOU* began again. In introductory frames waited the final moments of what he'd last read back in October, 1975, the day after Martin had gone missing. A fictional figure named Brady McCulough has come to stand in front of his comic-book bedroom door, frightened by noises issuing out of the room. Brady's hand reaches out to grasp the knob and turns it, opening the door into an artist's depiction of his bedroom.

When John turned the page to follow the succeeding set of frames, the face he saw next wasn't Brady's face. It was Martin's, illustrated by some demented artist, capturing the minute details of Martin's features...the freckles across the bridge of his nose, a small mole on his chin.

"My God." He brought a hand up to his mouth as he studied how Martin had looked back then, on the night he'd disappeared. Martin's face looking up in the next frame, hopeful, beckoning someone into the illustrated bedroom.

John retched as he turned the page, knowing what he would see next: himself as a boy, walking into Martin's room within this damned abandoned house. Each frame continued on, recapturing his nightmare of that fateful evening in a flurry of inks and dialogue boxes. Martin's bedroom window had been open, allowing in the cool evening breeze. It was...

☠   ☠   ☠

...letting too much wind into the room.

"You'd better shut that," John told Martin. "Dad isn't into heating the great outdoors."

Martin hailed him inside, excited. John hesitated. Martin's room always gave him the willies. Martin kept things in there which never failed to pre-empt a nightmare. A pale rubber Dracula mask dangled from a wire over Martin's bed, spinning in the wind, hollow eye sockets reflecting orange light from the nearby lamp. Rubber fangs quivered.

"Look at this," Martin held up a comic. *Authentic Horror Comics* it read, October issue, Volume 2, Issue 2. "Cool, huh?"

John regarded a drawing of a skull bearing strips of rotting flesh. "Gross."

Martin rocked with laughter. "Chicken, you almost whizzed yourself!"

"Did not." He wanted to run from Martin's room and felt ashamed at his reaction.

"It creeps up on you," John intoned, feigning boredom.

"What does? Old age? Those monsters of yours?"

"You have no imagination."

"You have too much of one," John shot back. "Why do you like this kind of stuff anyway?" He refrained from looking at the posters of film shots from *Creature from the Black Lagoon* and *Burnt*

Offerings. Martin had managed to find a publicity photo of Norman Bates standing on the steps of his *Psycho* house during the filming, the set full of cupolas and eaves jutting over his shoulder like dark wings. Mother? Enter the bleating music 'scree! scree! scree! scree' while a woman showers behind a closed curtain, a shower meant to be warm and comforting after a long drive, enveloping you in the steam of your own hot blood, curdling, rolling into a drain, looking tar-like in the grainy black-and-white picture.

"Real people playing make-believe is all it's about," Martin continued. "I always wished I could find a poster from *I Am Legend*."

"To add to your potpourri of madness," John finished. "I don't know how you can sleep in here, and I think you have a problem."

"It's cool to be scared." Martin's eyes shone with glee. "It's harmless thrills, John. Lighten up, you worry too much. Listen to the opening of this story."

John slumped against the doorway. "Hurry. I still have homework to do."

Martin broke into an enthusiastic narrative. "There's this kid named Brady. He bought the same issue of the comic I'm reading, and get this—he's reading the same story *IT CREEPS UP ON YOU*. This comic is about itself. Brady leaves his room to go the bathroom, but when he gets back the wind has blown his bedroom door shut. He hears something sliding around in there, bumping into walls...and he goes to open the door..."

Martin held up the frame of Brady's hand coming to rest on his doorknob before that fateful second of discovery.

"That's enough," John said. "Homework's calling my name."

Martin chuckled. "Chicken."

John started to retreat, then paused to glance back, bothered by something he couldn't pinpoint. "Where'd you find this comic anyway?"

Martin raised his eyebrows. "Smoke shop. Why?"

"I've never heard of it before."

"New one," Martin intoned, laying the comic across his lap. "I'm glad."

John nodded. "You're weird, Martin."

"And you're a chicken. Go and do your homework," Martin grinned.

John forced a smile and headed up the hallway.

☠   ☠   ☠

The evening was cold, dark, windy. John sat down at his desk, trying to find comfort in the small halo of gold light from his reading lamp. He found himself gazing through the window at the night-soaked street across from their house. It was almost Halloween and someone's plastic skeleton did a slow jig from a tree branch, arms and legs whirling, dark eyes and mouth flipping past.

He got up to shut his drapes and his breath caught in his throat as a shape surged at him from the other side of the glass...

...and let out the breath as he realized it was his own reflection caught in the lamp light.

He worked on algorithms. The wind picked up outside, scuttling dry leaves into gutters. Sounds from his parents' television program drifted up to him.

Something built up at the other end of the hallway, coming as a sensation, then changing in air pressure. It became a whistle of strong wind gaining momentum. Martin's door slammed shut with a vicious crack. He must have left his window open, except it felt like a hurricane now.

John lunged from his chair and ran toward Martin's door. Pale light squeezed out along the bottom of the frame. He thought he heard what sounded like a low, resonating chuckle, followed by the hollow cough of glass blowing out from a window.

"Martin?" he tried. His hand reached out for Martin's door handle and he was struck by the vision of deja-vu. He thought of the cartoon character, Brady, in the frame Martin had held up for him to see. A boy's hand resting on a door knob...

Wind tickled at his legs and footsteps from below started up the stairs.

John twisted the door handle and shoved the door open. He got sucked into the room, the window blown all the way out, exposing the crisp night beyond the house. A venetian blind tumbled around, suspended by its cords, then let go with a hard, ripping sound.

Martin stood in front of the ruined window, his long blond hair drawn back from his skull so that it distorted the shapes of his eyelids. He reached out with both hands for John.

"Help me," he mouthed and his lips shimmied in the force. John saw something move in, looking like night and smoke and fog, vaporous, twisting around Martin's legs and waist. Dark greens, reds, golds, black lines undulated and merged like chimerical snakes in water. Martin's eyes were dark, wide holes of pleading. His voice began to break up like a distant radio signal, echoing to the left, to the right, then fading out altogether. Then he was sucked out through the window, enwrapped in the colors, and disappeared.

John couldn't move his feet. He was awake yet launched in the sticky, sedentary surrealism of dreamland, unable to react. His eardrums popped. For a second he saw Martin's eyes. They shone like dull, wet globes in the dark. The *Authentic Horror Comic* tumbled from the bed, rolling end over end until it crushed itself against a far wall.

Something grabbed John from behind and he shrieked.

"Where's your brother?"

"I...don't know." He collapsed. When he woke it was to find himself in the pristine surroundings of a hospital ward, pressed between sheets. He dreamt of open windows, of wind, and of pumpkins gutted like whistles in the emptiness of October evenings. He'd scream and someone would come and sedate him again. The dreams would fade to the grateful hum of white snow blowing across the screen of his numb mind.

☠   ☠   ☠

Part of the address remained on the house, a *2* hanging from one nail by the front door. A wad of rain-soaked flyers lay in a mouldy pile at the base of the door, near his parents old black, galvanized mailbox. A bird had made a nest inside. It lay dead on its side, eye sockets dried to raisins.

The comic frames in the edition he now held had continued the story about the missing person's report John's parents had filed with the police; the agony of waiting for Martin's return. It continued like a twisted autobiography, covering him growing up without a big brother, attending college without Martin, the death of his parents years later...

"Sick piece of crap!" He kept reading, despite himself. Next frame, a scene from a antiquated pawn shop.

He bent over and threw up. The comic was retracing his steps this morning…he thumbed past the next few pages to find unfinished frames, yet to be drawn.

Moving back to the continuation of the story, he saw himself looking at himself in illustrated form, where a man wearing his clothing stands on a front porch, a number two dangling from the wall.

He glanced at the windows, the overbearing trees, seeking a camera-obscura. Nothing but the bleak sky stared back.

He turned the page. A dark figure looks down at his illustrated self from inside Martin's old bedroom.

He leapt from the porch and ran into the backyard to locate Martin's old window. Broken glass filled with spider webs stared indifferently into the yard. He saw nothing move in there. His parents had repaired the room, sold the house, then the house had continued to sell, be bought, sold again…finally abandoned. It looked beaten.

Last frame of the story in his hands before the blank squares began: *TO BE CONTINUED.*

He swayed in the overgrown grass, feeling vertigo. He came to rest beside a forgotten oil tank reeking of old fuel.

It would go wherever he decided to take it today. Some dark magic controlled the drawing pen.

He imagined the way the house had looked back then. He snapped back to reality. The house smelled dead, full of dust, mildew, bird shit, stagnant air and time. He wrapped his coat around his hand and smashed the glass from the back, then stepped into the kitchen. He whirled and heard a muted 'pop' in the room, coming somewhere from above his head. Colors brightened from time, or faded: plums merging into reds, mosses into brilliant greens, hard yellows into soft russets, black lines diminishing to the shadows of the corners. He sucked in his breath. There to his left was their old breakfast nook, its benches wiped clean with lemon oil, a checkered tablecloth anointing its surface. Salt and pepper shakers and a sugar bowl sat propped against one wall. Beside them waited an open box of Count Chocula cereal…Martin's favorite.

"Martin," he whispered. He spun in slow motion. Even the floor was clean and waxed. A stove waited, a pot simmering on a burner. Lace curtains hung over the windows. His mother had sewn them. He could see her wash hanging on the line; it contained his old denim overalls, Martin's football shirts, rows of socks from their grade school years.

He turned and stepped through the kitchen archway towards the parlor. A television screen flickered. The back of a sofa with the gentle arcs of his parents' heads rested against cushions.

Another 'pop' and his ears rang. The parlor image blinked out like a flash cube glare and the parlor returned to murk, dust, newspaper chewed into rodent nests. He glanced back at the kitchen. No light, no simmering meal, no lemon oil. Cobwebs clung to the archway. The back door with its broken window mocked him.

He squeezed the comic in his hand. He wanted to hurt it, but more, he wanted to see where it might go.

John, over here.

The voice issued from the direction of the bedrooms.

He mounted the stairs, gripping the handrail, kicking dust up in high, grey plumes. He stopped at the landing and gritted his teeth— Martin's old bedroom door sat shut—but that oh-so-pale slice of citron slipped out from the gap near the bottom, filling the hall with a dusting of ethereal light.

He felt himself move forward, felt his arm reach out for the familiar knob. He gripped the comic in the other hand. Martin's door blew open on a gust of stale wind.

☠   ☠   ☠

He stood in the doorway of Martin's bedroom once again. A lamp was lit on a side table. The bed neatly made. The rubber Dracula mask, whirled, grinning at him. Anthony Perkins darkened the step of his *Psycho* house.

The door bucked against him. Something moved behind it.

"Martin?" he screamed.

"Not yet." The voice carried in the stagnant air. It was deep, aged, weary.

A man stepped out from behind the door. He looked very real. His hair was yellow-white and streaked with rusty strands of copper. He wore a wool cardigan and brown pants. Gold hairs shone along the backs of his hands. He smelled like old books.

"Who the hell are you?" John gripped the comic, wishing he'd brought something heavy with him instead...a flashlight, a tire iron...

The man's eye's burned an unreal green.

"I was a boy who liked these infernal comics, too. I'm sorry, John to have done this. I want you to put yourself in my shoes—try and understand. I wanted to come back home. I needed Martin. Do you know who I am? Surely, by now you must have some idea."

John fell back against he door frame, winded. "No...you aren't real. Brady?"

The old man gave a painful nod. "As real as Martin once was, and still can be, if you're willing to make a sacrifice. There are no answers, only solutions. How much do you want your brother back? How much are you willing to give up? It must be enough if you've come home, looking for ghosts."

John regarded him. All color had washed from his face. "I don't follow you."

Brady took a step forward. "The comic you hold isn't a regular publication, but you already know that. It has it's own purpose. You never married, did you?"

John glared. "What business is that of yours?"

"It isn't," Brady said. "Just observation. I had a sister who'd never married until later, when I came back. She brought my cursed copy of Part A *IT CREEPS UP ON YOU* to a smoke shop and left it on the magazine shelf. I'd been reading it before I disappeared. She wanted to get rid of it, wanted it far from the house. By the time Margaret left it at the smoke shop that October afternoon, I'd been gone for three years."

"Why didn't she just trash it?" John rasped, exasperated. "Why bring it to a store? It was second hand!"

"Because by then she knew."

"Knew what? You're not talking sense."

"Let me explain. These things...these comics, have their way of getting around, and it had been around before it had found me. It would go around again, waiting for the next burst of interest. Unfortunately, it was your brother, Martin who noticed it. I know, I was there, watching him purchase it. He was a dedicated reader."

John staggered. "You're saying he's been kept captive, maybe drugged somewhere, or institutionalized all these years? What have you done with him?"

"No," Brady shook his head. "Not institutionalized, but immortalized in print. In there, in that comic you hold in your hand. That's your key. You must find someone to replace Martin. Unfinished stories must go on. When one ends, another begins. It is the state we know as 'limbo'. I was in those pages, alive within the molecular folds of ink and paper and glue, watching Martin read about me, watching him show the comic to you...and how you'd backed away, not wanting to see any of it. I worried Martin might stop reading, might not reach the end of the section, but he did...he arrived at the part where I needed someone to open their bedroom door and begin a new scene. In that moment I was released and it waited for him to fill my place.

"How many people have disappeared over time, never to be found? Police files gone cold?"

"You're saying these comics exist to serve some dark purpose?"

Brady leveled his gaze. "I've seen what magic can do, when you believe in the story. Be afraid of the Dracula mask, John. Beware of night things and the unexplained. I've felt your terror all these years, working through this town, centering its core in this house, the nucleus of your emotion and the focal point of my escape. You came back because you never stopped wanting to see your brother again. My sister did it for me. I can't blame you for what you're about to do."

"I returned because I found this comic in a store this morning," John said vehemently. "It was pure chance, nothing else."

"No," Brady shook his head. "It knew you would. It needs fresh blood. Martin is running low, like a battery sucked dry. The story requires a fresh angle, a continuity of situation, a new...character. Take it back to a store where you found it, John. Place it on a shelf. Don't let anyone interfere with your plan. Ensure someone else...someone with a passion for this kind of story, buys it. When they do and begin to read it, you'll know. So will Martin. You'll feel an urge to return to this house once more, and you will find him here. I promise it. Now go. You'll never see me again; I've done my part. Martin's time will come when he will do the same for someone else. I'm sorry, I was only a boy back then. I didn't know any differently. Neither did he."

Brady turned and passed into the hallway. John stepped out to watch him go, but Brady had vanished. No footsteps, no passage of wind, no echo of a door being opened downstairs. Pop! He clapped both hands to his ears. Martin's bedroom had changed again. It was back to being dusty, the window boarded over, the room forgotten in time.

The comic tickled at his hand.

☠   ☠   ☠

John brought the *Authentic Horror Comic*, with his brother Martin contained within its pages to another used book store called *Second Time Around*. He sold it for a quarter. A bell tinkled as John pocketed the money and he turned to regard the people entering the store. A young mother and her boy about eight years old moved into the room. The mother began leafing through a table full of romance novels. The boy left her side.

"Oh neat!" the boy said, noticing John's comic on the counter. "Can I have it, Mom?"

John felt his stomach recoil. This child was so young...maybe seven, eight years old. He wanted to yell at the boy to drop the damning comic. Then he thought of Martin. How badly did he want to see Martin again? He had to know if Brady's words could come true.

"Danny, those kinds of things don't appeal to me," his mother said.

"I love them," the boy pleaded. "Please, how much is it?"

"Fifty cents," said the proprietor, looking at John and winking. "Good deal if you ask me."

The woman sighed and gave the boy a dollar to purchase the comic.

John turned and left the store, tears in his eyes. He hoped Martin would help Danny years from now. He ached for Danny's mother, then realized that his own mother had never had a choice against powers beyond her understanding.

He never looked back. He drove to his house on Parson's Road. It was sunset, cool, windy as he left the car. He crossed the street and watched the lawn fill with autumnal leaves slick with frost. He heard a 'pop', looked back, and saw that his car was gone, replaced instead by a 60's Chevy Impala and a Volkswagen Beetle. He looked down and saw that he wore the runners his mother had bought him the summer he'd graduated from grade five. Old Adidas. There was the wash strung out on the line. He stepped onto the porch, noting the clean window hung with a white lace curtain, and pushed open the door. The smell of cooking came to him. His ears popped.

Today Martin would walk to a smoke shop to peruse the magazine stands for something to read and things would happen differently. John would go with him. He would find the Authentic Horror Comic first and hide it well away from Martin's view. Let the boy in the Second Time Around have a go of it, do his time, and release Martin Ingram to his life again. Right now was all that mattered. They were being given a second chance. It didn't matter how or why.

A shiver touched his flesh as he made his way towards the parlor where his parents and Martin watched television. He told himself it was just the October chill, and went to greet them.

Noises Off: Behind The Screams

IF YOU are not one who likes to get the story behind the story or "see the strings" behind the play and absolutely never watch the special features on a DVD where you can listen to commentary by the director, actors, writers, etc., then I suggest that you stop here. I doubt you would enjoy what is about to come. But I do want to thank you for coming this far with me. I hope that you enjoyed your experience and didn't mind the silent screams.

However, if you're one who is willing to walk along with the author and listen to some of the details behind the stories and poems that appear in this collection, then grab your jacket. It's a damp night with a full moon. There's a cool wind from the north and we've got a long walk ahead of us. Let me bend your ear as you and I engage in a little jaunt.

☠   ☠   ☠

About The Cover

THE COVER design for this book was done by Steve Gaydos, a very talented graphic designer from Ottawa and someone whom I've been fortunate enough to count among my dearest friends for more than half of my life. Steve put together something that has a strong personal meaning to me and which I find absolutely stunning. Having always been inspired by M. C. Escher's strange and wonderful body of work, I expressed to Steve my fondness for the cover being reminiscent of that. I've always found Escher's work intriguing and sometimes on the verge of disturbing. Steve captured that feeling wonderfully in an ode to Escher's "Eye" (1946).

For the cover, Steve was also able to incorporate a charcoal sketch of a skull that my wife Francine's maternal grandmother Agnes Bartlett drew in 1938 when she was in art school. I never had the pleasure of meeting this wonderful lady, as she'd died a year before I met Francine. But I've heard how much she loved ghost stories, and how much she would have enjoyed reading my fiction. Many of her beautiful pieces of art hang in several rooms of our home, (the skull, of course, hangs near my writing space) and I am honoured to be able to use her work for my cover.

The author photo, which appears on the back cover, was taken by another lifelong friend, Greg Roberts. A self-taught photographer, Greg has a great eye and a knack for making the most beautiful photos look simple and "easy" matching his easygoing, straightforward and consistently dependable nature. Although he's one of the most intelligent and technically accomplished people I've known, he's never been pretentious about it and has always used his powers for good, not evil. His work can be enjoyed on his website at www.gregrob.ca.

Browsers
First Published in <u>Challenging Destiny</u> #5, January 1999

IT'S NO accident that I wanted this story to lead the collection. Because so much of my life has involved surrounding myself with books, this is a tale that is still very close to my heart. That I could combine my passion for books with a "Twilight Zone" type of tale was a very satisfying exercise. I'm also tickled by the fact that I was able to build in a reference to one of my favourite novels, <u>Earth Abides</u> by George R. Stewart.

This tale was inspired by one of my own quests to explore used bookstores in a "strange" city. At the time, Francine and I were living in Ottawa and were visiting her mother in Hamilton. While mother and daughter made plans to go on an all-day shopping expedition I decided to go on my own little quest. I took the Yellow Pages and a map of the city and made a note of all the book and magazine shops in the area. I then set out to visit them all.

It was during this trip that I encountered the used bookstore that inspired this tale. It appeared to be a small corner shop, but inside it was an interesting catacomb of inter-connected rooms that seemed to go on forever. One of the "rooms" and shelves were in the middle of being built while I wandered through the shop, but my imagination had already spawned its own ideas of how new rooms were constructed here.

I purposely didn't name the narrator, nor identify their sex. My goal was not just to allow the reader to identify with this book lover but to be able to step directly into their role, whether they themselves were male or female. The only indication that I was successful with this was when I saw the illustrations by Janet Chui, which appeared with my story in <u>Challenging Destiny</u>. Janet picked up on this subtle cue and kept up the masquerade – her excellent illustrations, perfectly matching the mood and sense of mystery I'd intended, didn't reveal the narrator's face and, in a long flowing overcoat, allowed the narrator to remain asexual. Thanks Janet.

Distractions
Previously unpublished in print. First appeared in <u>World Fantasy Con 2001 CD-ROM</u> edited by Nancy Kilpatrick

WRITING, BEING a completely self-directed activity requiring steadfast determination and unwavering commitment, is often the first activity to be sacrificed to make room for other activities. In other words, it's easy to let distractions become a convenient excuse as to why I'm not writing.

While attempting to work at identifying a list of distractions in the hopes of eliminating them prior to my "writing time" (likely advice I'd gathered from one of the many writing guides or magazines that I continue to read every year), I mused that I was acting like a self-help guru. I began to wonder what a book hot off the "self-help" shelves on eliminating distractions might be called and who the author might be.

Then, I imagined a frustrated author embracing the book and taking its simple message to new extremes.

In 2001, Nancy Kilpatrick sent a communication to a list of Canadian writers of science fiction, fantasy and horror, looking for submissions to a CD-ROM that would be given out at the World Fantasy Convention being held in Montreal that year. She was looking for stories, poems and essays retrospective of past WF Con themes while featuring Canadian talent.

One of the categories that hadn't been filled was the "Fantasy Writers of the Southwest" theme. To match the requirements for this theme, I re-wrote "Distractions" further fleshing out my main character from a "could live anywhere" writer to a fantasy writer living in the Southwest.

From Out of the Night
First published in <u>The Darker Woods</u> #2, February 1997

THIS IS one of my earlier attempts at writing that survived and graduated from my own personal slush pile.

I was in my mid-teens when one evening my mother was frantically dashing through the house closing curtains and turning off the lights. A group of Jehovah's Witnesses were canvassing the neighbourhood, but my mother was acting like this was Nazi Germany or perhaps there were flesh-eating zombies on the loose.

The original story that I wrote was simply an attempt to play with this simple fear and stopped at the "punch-line" that after all the fuss and bother, it was merely those religious people. The story was about 800 words. I began to think of the story in terms of science fiction and wondered what it might be like if society became so science-oriented that basic religions were seem as cult-type activities from the "dark ages." I introduced Mary's husband who was a writer and had him introducing and concluding the story. The opening and closing remarks that John writes were an attempt to pay tribute to Rod Serling's "Twilight Zone" as well as all the books on Bigfoot, the Lock Ness Monster, UFO's and other unexplainable paranormal activity that I'd voraciously absorbed for years.

By then the story ran a little over 1000 words. But I wasn't entirely satisfied. I wanted to explore why John let his wife carry on the charade. I wanted to understand how a husband could just "let it go" without a concern for helping his wife.

Then, drawing details from my own faith, I made the unmentioned religion Roman Catholicism. I drew parallels between the beliefs of my faith and vampirism (life everlasting, the sacrament of Holy Communion), and worked at making the pretence of Mary's fear a little more frightening.

I also explained what might happen if, to protect her family, Mary took matters into her own hands and greeted the callers with a knife. John would realize, too late, his mistake.

The editor who published the story in The Darker Woods #2, Stephanie Connolly offered some fantastic comments and suggestions that helped me polish the story up. In 1996, when I'd originally sent the story, she liked the concept and the tension, but she offered ideas for a re-write that helped bring the characters and point of view home. I was able to use her suggestions to re-write the tale. The one thing that she didn't like about the re-write was the bloody ending. She felt it didn't add to the story, and, when she published it, she left that part out.

Not that I don't respect this editor's judgement – she helped me further realize the John/Mary relationship at a whole new depth and I do feel that she made the right choice for her magazine – but once the story was published, I continued to re-write the tale so that the bloody ending had a maximum impact. I focused on how seeing the blood-covered Mary was the final straw in John realizing the grave way that he'd failed his wife, by allowing her neurosis to go unchecked. I feel I brought that home, finally, when he simply walks over and holds his wife. This character realization became crucial to the resolution of the story.

Nervous Twitching
First published in <u>NorthWords</u> Fall 1996 Issue, November 1996

THIS IS just a short vignette attempting to parallel the "chicken running around with its head cut off" concept with a similar thing happening to a human. Why does the hero of the tale kill his lover? With it out of misguided passion, a spurned lover's revenge, or did he simply snap and re-enact a childhood chicken-beheading episode that he'd kept repressed all these years?

I honestly don't know. I thought it best to leave the answers to those questions up to the reader.

I like this story because in a short space it sends the reader into a surrealistic disturbing scene.

The Bogeyman Can
First published in <u>imelod</u> Vol 4, #4, January 1999

DURING A writing warm-up exercise I'd scribbled the "Bogeyman Can" lyrics to the tune of "The Candyman Can" – writing poetry in a spoofing fashion often got my creative muscles pumped. I think it's something about the exercise of getting new words or meanings fit in to the same rhythm and beat of a known structure that works well for me.

Whatever inspired me to try to turn this quick lyric generation into a tale that gave them a setting is lost to me, now. But I did it, and I had fun fleshing out the conflict between the artsy Rogers and the uptight Martin – judge for yourself whether or not I should have simply just left it at the silly poetry.

Almost
Previously unpublished

"ALMOST" IS the classic "tale of the hook", of an escaped convict on the loose (notable, of course, for the "hook" in the place of a hand) and of a pair of young lovers out in their car looking for a night of passion.

Virtually hundreds of takes on this story exist. Over the years I have read (or heard around campfires) many different versions of this tale, but I hadn't yet heard it from the point of view of the escaped convict. This story was my attempt at that.

The Sound of One Man Screaming
Previously unpublished

THIS ONE was written specifically with this collection in mind. I wanted to try to capture and express my view of the world. I wrote this while tucked between my desk and computer table using the standard desk props, which all appear in the poem, as my inspiration.

You might suggest having me committed, but I think it nicely captures what it is that actually occurs when I'm writing.

Frost After Midnight
First published in <u>NorthWords</u> Fall 1996 Issue, November 1996

WHILE STUDYING for an exam for my English Romantic Writers course at Carleton University, I needed a "let loose" break. I often found myself most creative or most inspired to write a story while taking such a study break. One time I wrote a 20 minute "screenplay" spoofing <u>Star Trek: The Next Generation</u> called "Star Trek: The Generation After The Next" which my friend John Ellis and I shot on a VHS camera in the space of an afternoon, playing all 10 characters in the script in my Baba's basement apartment in Levack during Christmas vacation, using clothes around the house for costumes and sound and special effects from an old Intellivision game system. But that particular burst of energy was a bit rare. Most of the time, I simply wrote a short story or a poem.

Given that Coleridge's work was in front of me that afternoon, and the fact that I love his "Frost At Midnight" with its wonderful time freeze snapshot of one man's midnight musings, I couldn't help but wonder if, elsewhere, in a darker region of the universe, a sick and evil mind might not be having similar, yet more morbid musings.

With Apologies To E. P.
First published in <u>Twisted Devotion</u> #1, April 1999

HAVE I mentioned how much I enjoy parodies of works that I respect and admire? Is imitation the sincerest form of flattery? My favourite Elvis Presley song is "Are You Lonesome Tonight?" most likely because of the parallels that Elvis draws between his failed love affair and the theatre. The title was also a tribute to the titles that the Romantic poets sometimes used whenever the poem they were writing touched upon a subject or made reference to something another poet had produced.

'Nuff said? (And yes, dear reader, that phrase is a purposeful nod to Mr. Stan Lee, creator of Spider-Man and the first writer whose own great stories inspired me to want to tell my own tales of imagination)

There Is A Low And Fearful Cry
First published in <u>NorthWords</u> Fall 1996 Issue, November 1996

THIS IS another poem that I wrote while studying the English Romantic Poets in University. Wow, looking back, it seems like I studied a lot to have taken so many study breaks, doesn't it? I was attempting to write something that reflected delving into the self, into the very matter of fear and trying to leave the reader with an ominous feeling.

The Romantic poets and Poe could pull this off while using a tight rhyming structure that I don't often see used today in serious poetry. I wonder if it still works today for anyone besides me. I love this one, placing it somewhere on par with my Coleridge spin-off.

Blood Dreams
First published in <u>NorthWords</u> Fall 1996 Issue, November 1996

DO MURDERERS have blood dreams? Are they haunted by the images of wrongs and crimes they have committed? Like "With Apologies To E.P." and perhaps in allusion to Poe's "The Tell-Tale Heart" this poem explores the guilty mind of a killer.

Wailin' Jenny
First published in <u>Thin Ice</u> XV, May 1994

THIS IS another one of those writing warm-up spoofs that I was having fun with – this time I had a go at a classic country music song and used the title to make reference to a country music singer's name. I'm not sure why I thought it would be cute to write short rhyming verse about cannibalism, but this is just one of many short sick verses that I wrote.

Holiday Demons
First published in <u>Crossroads</u> #16, October 1996

This was another look at a twisted/distorted mind, perhaps similar to the mind of "Mary" in "From Out of the Night" but this time in poetry format. I often find myself plagiarising from my own work. This usually happens when the idea won't go away, perhaps because I hadn't worked with it enough – perhaps because I had another way of getting the idea out there.

I debated over whether I should put this "Halloween" poem with the three other Halloween tales in this collection, but decided to let format rule over theme.

Phantom Mitch
First published in <u>Wicked Mystic</u> #22, October 1993

THIS STORY went on to receive honourable mention in **The Year's Best Fantasy & Horror** #7 edited by Datlow and Windling. Getting the short typewritten note in my SASE from Ellen Datlow was quite a thrill, despite the fact that I didn't initially know what it meant. In my submissions journal I made the following note. ". . . received note from Ms. Datlow . . . 'Phantom Mitch' made her 'rec' list for 1993. (Wonder what that means)." At the time I didn't know what that was, and when the book came out, I got a second thrill when I saw my name on the "honourable mention" list on the same page with Richard Laymon. Thanks for that amazing double thrill Ms. Datlow.

(I'm going to take an aside here, and pause to tell you that if you are a horror fan and you haven't experienced a Richard Laymon novel, you're missing out on something great. When I was working at a bookstore in Ottawa, I used to offer to personally buy back a copy of Laymon's "In The Dark" or "One Rainy Night" if the buyer wasn't completely satisfied. I never had any takers. Get the picture? Richard is no longer with us – he died unexpectedly on Feb 14, 2002 – but he left this world a much richer place with his writing. So get out there, get your hands on as many of his works as you can and read them.)

The story basically explores the concept of amputees experiencing an itch on their "phantom" extremity (ie, feeling an itch between the toes on a leg that was amputated). What if the itch was real because the phantom extremity actually still existed, but on another plane? What if you could touch a dead loved-one with that phantom limb?

In an early version of this story, it was a chilling horror tale with Barry's wife an evil vengeful dead wife coming back to get even with him for killing her in the accident. The story was called "Phantom Bitch." I liked the play on words. The story didn't do much for me, though, so I re-wrote it as a love story. Wanting to keep the play on words in the title, I changed Barry's wife's name to Michelle. I think I ended up with a much better story and a much tighter play on words. Sometimes it's the little things that keep me amused.

Erratic Cycles
First published in <u>Parsec</u> Vol 3, No 2, February 1999

HAVING GROWN up in the small town of Levack which is located north of Sudbury and off Highway 144 in Northern Ontario, I developed what I think is a natural and healthy fear of the formidable *King's Highway*. But it wasn't really the highway that frightened me – it was the wilderness and "unknown" which the highway snaked through which captured my fearful imagination.

I originally created this tale as a "ghost car" tale about our hero's car breaking down, then getting picked up by a phantom car that forever repeats it's fatal accident, only this time taking our story's hero along with him. At the time the story was called "Compact Car" – after spending about 3 hours one lonely night during my first year of University composing this tale on my Commodore 64 computer (do you remember those?), I somehow lost the entire file when a static-electric shock fried my system. That was my first lesson in the importance of backing up important computer files to disc. The Commodore 64 of course didn't even have a hard drive or a "temp" folder, so if you didn't create a floppy disc (or tape) backup, and you lost power, your work was toast. Too stubborn to abandon this tale, I attempted to re-write and re-create it that same night. There went another 3 hours. (Something in the back of my head still tells me that the second version wasn't quite as good as the first – I don't know, maybe there's just something special about your first time)

A couple of re-writes and rejections later, it became apparent that I threw two conflicting supernatural elements into one story and they didn't make sense together. Also, it was blatantly obvious, almost from the beginning of the tale, that the car picking up Charles was a ghost car and that the driver was already dead. Thus I ditched the idea of the ghost car and focused more on the fear of the encroaching forest. After all, it has been that fear which had originally inspired me to start writing this tale.

That decision allowed me to develop the concept of the childhood tale of the "Bush People" which sounded, to me, like the tales that parents might make up to scare their children into behaving a specific way. This version of the story was titled "The Forest For The Trees."

A couple of rejections later, I understood that I hadn't properly developed my main character. So he's alone in the middle of nowhere and scared because of some childhood fantasy tale about the "Bush People." Why should the reader care? I began peeling away at the onion of his background. Who was he? Why was he really afraid of being alone? What was he running from and why did being alone force him into facing that? When I started to answer those questions, this started to become a real story.

The title became "Erratic Cycles" and Parsec accepted the story in April 1997. It was published in 1999. While Charles never got to his intended destination, the story finally got to its own.

After it was published, the story then went on to be nominated for an Aurora Award for Best Short-Form Work In English. Robert J. Sawyer ended up winning the award that year, but I was honoured to have my work listed alongside writers whose work I respected.

Also, during the Aurora Awards ceremony, I was sitting between Don Hutchison and Don Bassie who both took home Aurora Awards that day. Don H. took home the award for his work on editing **Northern Frights** (and, incidentally, had been one of the editors who rejected the story but offered insightful, useful comments that helped me to make it better. Thanks, Don). Don B. won the award for his work on the Made in Canada website which promotes science fiction, fantasy and horror written by Canadians. It was almost as exciting to be the first person to congratulate each of these friends as they won their awards as it would have been to win – almost!

What I find important about this story's genesis (like that of "From Out of the Night") is that it illustrates how, with a lot of work, determination, and actually listening to constructive criticism from very knowledgeable people, a writer can take a trite piece of writing and flesh it out, fully realize the characters and the story, and come up with something not half bad.

Requiem
First published in Darkness Within #2, October 1999

"REQUIEM" WAS inspired by "true" ghost stories that some bookseller colleagues of mine and I were talking about between serving customers and shelving books at the Coles at St. Laurent Shopping Centre in Ottawa. We began talking about haunted places, when one of my colleagues recounted a tale of a haunted mirrored bureau or cabinet. Apparently, strange things happened when the antique was moved into someone's home and then one family member wouldn't return to the room the bureau was in because when she looked into the mirror she'd seen the reflection of this little girl dressed in Victorian clothes looking back.

The tale, while giving me chills, also called further concepts and questions to mind. The first was that objects, not just houses could be haunted. The second was the idea of a haunted mirror showing an image of the ghost haunting it. So what if the mirror could also reveal other ghosts? And what if those ghosts had all been thrust together by a collector who collects haunted objects?

I began drafting up what I imagined would be a man who would do such a thing. He was elite, French, rich and eclectic – he was a loner who lived off of his parent's wealth in a large mansion by himself. He was paranoid about the outside world, yet fascinated by the supernatural.

Suddenly, I'd found an easy way to isolate my main character – a malfunctioning "black market" security system. After all, the common problem with many ghost stories is not having a clear answer as to why the character doesn't just leave when signs of the ghost first show up? In this case, Peter wanted to see the ghosts – but I had to be able to explain why, after he is frustrated with the endless quarrelling of the ghosts, he didn't just leave? His aversion to the outside world might be enough, but it certainly didn't satisfy me. I considered developing his aversion of people and the outside world into a full-blown phobia, but that would have changed the entire opening sequence. So a little illegally developed security system seemed to fit the bill.

A few years later, and shortly after this tale was published, I went out to dinner with a friend, Peter Halasz, who I'd met in one of the local science fiction circles. Peter is a voracious reader and a collector of Canadian speculative work. I knew he must be extremely well read because he had actually heard of me – it's not as if my writing was in easy-to-find publications. Most of my stories at that point had appeared in smaller press U.S. publications that couldn't be found on magazine stands in Canada; they could only be found in specialty shops or ordered direct from the publisher. Apart from being well read and thus having a discerning nature about quality writing and stories, Peter is difficult to impress. He is known for his extremely frank and honest nature, which is one of the things that I respect him for. He won't say that something I wrote was good or enjoyable if he didn't actually believe so just to be nice or pad a writer's ego. He doesn't waste time playing those games. Maybe other writers don't like that quality in a person, preferring to have their ego stroked, but I find Peter's honesty refreshing. If Peter does offer praise, you know it's not being given lightly and it therefore has much more meaning. I get enough of the "oh, it was nice" about my writing and I'd much rather have an in-depth conversation about why the writing didn't work, why it sucked or how it failed the reader in some way than any hollow praise. (Of course, an in depth: "Here's what I loved and found fascinating about your writing" is a much-preferred alternative, but one has to be realistic while being hopeful).

During our discussion, Peter did praise my ability to tell a story – my pace, timing and, in general, my readable style. In a nutshell, he said I was a good storyteller; but I wasn't a great writer. He illustrated his point by showing me where my writing got lazy, where I didn't pick the best possible way of describing something, or if I simply cheated by filling scenes with stereotypical or ill researched details. Again, I have to express that while hearing such frankness was not entirely pleasant, I was delighted that Peter was willing to take the time to walk through the story with me, and ecstatic that he cared enough to peel down to the really stinky part of the onion all for the benefit of helping me become a better writer.

One of the first issues that Peter pointed out was the way I'd described the auctioneer. I'd never been to a "gentleman's auction" and seen the way that such an event was carried out. Instead, I inserted the stereotypical country auctioneer often seen in television and movies. Peter had me corned. Yes, I had taken a shortcut in research and thus began the story with a blatant error. When including this tale in this collection, I considered changing that detail, but I ended up keeping it out of "poetic licence." Although I was technically incorrect, I liked the way I had described the auctioneer's spiel, and since it was such a short scene, I wondered if the average reader wouldn't catch the detail. Maybe it's my impression of our media-based society and the easy lies that television and movies immerse us in that we accept unquestioningly, but I thought I'd try to get away with it again. Besides, there is also the thought that I should be as true to the originally published work as possible.

While I did re-edit some of the sloppy wording and original phrase choices I'd used in the original version of this story, I did purposely leave a few of the gaffs Peter had pointed out in there for similar reasons that I justified to myself. Peter, I hope you understand. In any case, I'm sure we will have a fruitful and interesting discussion about it one day.

That Old Silk Hat They Found
First published in <u>Strange Wonderland</u> #1, March 1997

Ides of March
Previously unpublished

"THAT OLD Silk Hat They Found" is one of those tales that had been inspired entirely by a previously written story of mine: "Ides of March". It was in the early 1990's when I was living in Ottawa and I heard a radio news blurb about a man somewhere in the U.S. who'd been shot by someone who proceeded to steal his snowman. I wondered what kind of a person would shoot another person to steal a snowman, and it occurred to me: a person who thought perhaps, that by stealing the snowman and bringing them north to a colder climate, he could help them escape spring and what would be certain death. Kind of like an environmentalist risking his life to save a helpless baby seal from needless slaughter.

But that still wasn't enough, I felt, to make it really interesting. What if the "man" who stole the snowman was actually a snowman himself – on a mission to save as many of his kind as possible? I wrote the story and called it "Ides of March" (March 15th being a date not only thought of as a type of literary D-Day thanks to the warning given to Julius Caesar, but also a time when spring-type weather is likely to intensify).

This story was told from the point of view of a middle-aged man doing his taxes. The tale starts as he witnesses, through the window, two burly men in long jackets shoving at the neighbour's kid and stealing his snowman. I liked the tale, but not enough. I wrote it and only half heartedly sent it out to a few markets, then relegated it to my own personal slush pile (yes, in this case the pun is completely intended).

After a short period of time I considered re-telling one of the premises of the tale (the thought of associating spring with The Apocalypse was still intriguing to me); this time I did it from the snowman's point of view. As I began to write the tale I made the snowman a sentient narrator, and the narrator's voice began to take over the story, describing what it was like to wake up and find oneself to be a snowman. Inspired partly by Frankenstein's monster, who didn't ask to be "born" and partly by wanting to make a statement about the self-imposed God complex of humanity in general, I kept up this train of thought – what would it be like to be a snowman? How would a snowman think and feel about its circumstances? What would their "life" be like and what would an expected "lifespan" be? What tales would they tell? Culturally and anthropologically speaking, what legends of Genesis and Armageddon would they pass along to each other? Spring, and the cruel humans who selfishly created this "life" were the enemies as the narrator faced his darkest fears.

I'm particularly fond of the title as it calls upon the happy and innocent mystique of the children's song "Frosty The Snowman" and turns on the reader when they encounter what I felt would be a more realistic experience of a snowman coming to life . . .

Being a Northern Ontario boy at heart, and partial to all things *snow*, is it any wonder that I had to write at least two horror stories about snowmen?

But Once A Year
First published in <u>Crossroads</u> #13, October 1995

FRANCINE AND I were driving through upstate New York one fall, not far from the town of Black River where, Ken Abner, the editor of <u>Terminal Fright</u> magazine lived. At one point we passed a convenience store/gas bar across the street from a graveyard, and my mind started to take me to a fun place. I'd sent a few stories to Ken and he'd liked most of them, but my stories hadn't sufficiently raised his shackles. My original goal with this location-based inspiration was to write a tale that Ken might find a little familiar and close to home.

By the time I was finished writing the tale, I didn't think it really fit the type of story that Ken actually put into <u>Terminal Fright</u> so I never ended up sending it to him. But I did think that Pat Nielson, the editor of <u>Crossroads</u> would like it, given her soft spot for dark humour, Halloween and tales involving legends about crossroads.

I liked toying with the evil nature of cigarettes and how they played a part in a blatant betrayal of friendship. If there's any question about whether or not I was trying to make a statement about cigarettes and the tobacco industry, let me resolve it now – I certainly was.

I also enjoyed the ironic title for this story, as, at that point, it had been a year since I'd had my fiction in print, and, for two years in a row, they had been Halloween stories in Pat's magazine.

Treats
First published in <u>Crossroads</u> #19, October 1997

SPIDERS AND bugs scare the crap out of me. I know, I know, I'm 6' 3" and they are tiny little creatures – the creepy chill I get when something skitters out from beneath the freezer in the basement simply shouldn't occur. But it does. "Treats" was an attempt to write about this all-too familiar fear of bugs many of us have.

I thought I would approach the story with the idea of the fear of bugs being so strong in a person that it extended to fearing what would happen beyond death when they were buried. Wouldn't the bugs crawl into the coffin and get at their body? (Was this a natural extension of my own strange fear of being buried? – not buried alive, which is terrifying, but just the idea of being in a box 6 feet under the earth for the rest of eternity).

I imagined a man who so cherished his wife that, on her deathbed, he promised her that he wouldn't bury her, at least until the flesh was fully off of her bones. The rest of the story seemed to just roll together on its own momentum.

The rhyme from the kids came naturally enough – it's simply part of the script of childhood to pick a lonely hermit-like old person living on their street and spread rumours and stories about them regardless of any basis of fact, often making up some sort of nasty rhyme. The twist her, of course, is that there is some truth to their rhyme.

The story gave me the creeps. It freaked out my wife, who, believe it or not, is a little bit more scared of bugs than I am. It's hard to believe that anyone can scream louder and in a higher pitched voice when surprised by a bug than me, but it's true. Despite my own fear of creepy crawling critters, Francine regards me as the "bug eliminator" champion in our household. Even relative triumphs can be celebrated, no?

I walked away from this tale satisfied with having explored this fear and created a character in Percy that I really felt for.

Tricky Treater
First published in Crossroads #10, October 1994

I'M NOT exactly sure where the "Saint Anne" / "Satan" play on words first came to me. It was likely while my mind wandered, years ago, during a church service. I just knew, in the back of my mind, that one day I would use the idea in a story somewhere.

When considering a story for the magazine Crossroads: Where Evil Dwells, I read in Pat Nielsen's submission guidelines about her preference for stories involving crossroads, which was typically where encounters with evil occurred in many legends. The thought of a modern-day crossroads led me immediately to a convenience store on a city street, and Satan playing tricks on an unsuspecting store clerk.

I thought the premise was intriguing, and while this isn't one of my strongest stories, it's important to me as it was the story that initiated a great relationship with Editor Pat Nielsen, who published many of my stories, poems, artwork and reviews over the years. Thanks, Pat.

Til Death Do Us Part? (With John Strickland)
Previously unpublished

JOHN STRICKLAND was a co-worker who was also a writer, mentor and friend while I was employed as a theatre technician at Carleton University's Theatre Operations department in Ottawa. While it's been years since we've worked together or lived in the same city, I am fortunate enough to still count John as a mentor and a friend.

Back when I was still living in Ottawa, and still a single man with a lot of time on my hands, I would long for those rare stretches of time when John could get a "bachelor" day – in other words, when his wife, Renata, was out for the day visiting friends or family or running errands solo. On these "bachelor" days, John and I would get together and talk writing over a pot of coffee. Whenever the stretches of time were long enough, we'd try to create a story in "tag team" fashion.

With the pot of coffee and the word processor ready, John and I would take turns at the keyboard, each writing a paragraph or two, continuing on a round-robin type of story. We wouldn't discuss the tale; just tap the guy on the shoulder and say "your turn" whenever we got to a point that felt right. The one not writing would be relegated to another room listening to a classical music CD or CBC radio with a book in hand. When the story reached a mutually agreed upon point, we'd stop the changeover and read what we had written so far. Then we'd sit somewhere like on the back deck, with more coffee in hand, discuss the characters, the story's direction and decide on the story's plotline and resolution. Then we'd hammer out the ending and work together on a re-write.

Call me a writing nerd, but, short of spending a relaxing afternoon by the pool with my wife Francine, this is one of my favourite ways to spend an afternoon.

One of the things that I like best about writing with John is that, even now, when I look back on the stories we've written this way, I can't remember which of us wrote what scene. Our writing styles seem to have meshed wonderfully. I say this merely to elevate my view of my own writing, as John is an extremely talented writer.

John hasn't been actively writing since his daughter Emma was born in the mid 1990's, (so his writing is going to be relatively hard to find, at least for now) but I still hold every tale I write up to the "John Strickland" metre to see if it's any good. And I still try to do my mentor proud.

It Creeps Up On You (With Carol Weekes)
Previously unpublished in print. First appeared in <u>World Fantasy Con 2001 CD-ROM</u> edited by Nancy Kilpatrick

CAROL AND I met through a local Ottawa area online writer's discussion group. What we had in common was we were beginning writers in the Ottawa region with a passion for writing and for horror. What I wish we had in common was brilliant writing skill. Carol, you see, is a fantastically gifted writer. I am simply in awe of her writing ability and her commitment to excellence, and am honoured for the experience to have worked with her, both in writing projects as well as co-editing <u>Northern Fusion</u> magazine with her.

When her first novel sells, she is going to take the reading public (and the critics) by storm. People are going to wonder how she "came out of nowhere" without realizing the years of dedication, hard work and effort she put into her craft.

Carol and I wrote this tale a year or two after we met. We'd each begun the first several paragraphs of a story that we weren't sure where to go with next; as a fun exercise, we exchanged these stories to see if the other person would be able to do something with it. "It Creeps Up On You" was Carol's start that I added onto and flipped back to her. After several similar back and forth exchanges, the tale was finished and, similar to the experience I'd had with John Strickland on "Til Death Do Us Part?" we discussed the tale and elements (though entirely on the phone and via email, because we did this after I'd moved from Ottawa to Hamilton).

I get the feeling that this story will be my "claim to fame" for my association to Carol; that and <u>Northern Fusion</u> magazine. Carol is a humble, down to earth and genuine person who would be the first to refute my flattery of her work and talent. But I try to follow Peter Halasz's excellent example and not give praise lightly. My praise of

Carol's work is, without hesitation, completely warranted. You'd be doing yourself a favour, dear reader, to keep your eyes peeled for her writing. At the time of this writing, her short fiction can be found in **Northern Frights** 4 & 5, both edited by Don Hutchison, and both containing many other great tales of horror.

☠   ☠   ☠

Well that's the end of our walk, dear reader. I hope that I haven't been the only one to have enjoyed it. Thank you for joining me.

Writing is an interesting activity. While it's a deeply personal and self-involved activity, the act itself depends so much on the support, counsel and advice of many others: fellow authors, editors, friends, loved ones, as well as the works of countless writers that one admires and learns from just by reading. Once the writing is published, it depends on the right reader finding it, and hopefully, walking away from the experience with a little something more than they had when they first encountered it.

Dear reader, I hope that you were able to find something here to take away with you. Perhaps the memory of a short but pleasant escape from reality, an interesting character, a touching moment, an unexpected twist, or an unsettling chill; maybe just enough that you'll keep your eyes opened for some other writing by Mark Leslie. Perhaps you'll even be inspired enough to seek me out at a convention so we can engage in a similar jaunt, but this time where I listen to you.

So until we meet again, I bid you adieu.

About The Author

Mark Leslie Lefebvre was born in Sudbury, Ontario, in the late 1960's. He grew up in Levack, part of the town of Onaping Falls, about an hour's drive north of Sudbury where he attended Levack District High School. From there, he moved to Ottawa, where he attended Carleton University, achieved his B.A. Honours in English Language and Literature, and met his wife Francine. They married in 1996 and moved to Hamilton a year later. Their son, Alexander, was born in the summer of 2004.

Apart from writing fiction, Mark has published reviews of magazines and novels in various newspapers and magazines across North America. He also assistant edited NorthWords magazine, and co-edited Northern Fusion magazine with Carol Weekes. While continuing to write short fiction, Mark is completing work on his first novel *Morning Son*.

When he's not writing, Mark works in the I.T. department of Canada's largest bookseller at their home office in Toronto. He has been employed with them for over a decade, though in different guises. He started with Coles The Book People in Ottawa in the early 1990's – the company became Chapters in the mid 1990's, and in 2001 it became Indigo Books & Music. Over the years, the things that *have* remained consistent, were the great people he has worked with and of course, the books, always the books.